D1513929

JUST A SUMMER ROMANCE

When Lysette Dupont decides to help her grandfather restore his old windmill on Ile d'Oléron off the west coast of France, she doesn't want to get sidetracked into pursuing a deepening interest in the bohemian artist Xavier Monsigny. Xavier has planned to spend his time on the island painting and sketching — but intrigue and danger draw them into a summer romance . . . for, surely, that is all it will be?

KAREN ABBOTT

JUST A SUMMER ROMANCE

Complete and Unabridged

LINFORD
Leicester

First published in Great Britain in 2005

First Linford Edition
published 2006

British Library CIP Data

Abbott, Karen
    Just a summer romance.—Large print ed.—
Linford romance library
    1. Love stories
    2. Large type books
    I. Title
    823.9′14 [F]

    ISBN 1–84617–261–6

Published by
F. A. Thorpe (Publishing)
Anstey, Leicestershire

Set by Words & Graphics Ltd.
Anstey, Leicestershire
Printed and bound in Great Britain by
T. J. International Ltd., Padstow, Cornwall

This book is printed on acid-free paper

1

'No, it's quite impossible, dear!' Isabelle Cornaille said to her daughter, in tones that were clearly intended to end the argument without any further comment.

Her hand suspended for a fraction of a second as she flickered a glance at her daughter's face reflected in the mirror ... and then resumed its drawing of two finely-arched eyebrows over her cool grey eyes. Although now in her mid-forties, she was still a beautiful woman, and intended to stay that way, as her almost daily visits to the beauty salon bore out!

'But it's such a good opportunity, Maman,' Lysette Dupont argued. 'Danielle says we both stay in her uncle's house in Provence for a week or so and then we'll go to Italy and get some sort of summer job, which will give us time to look around before we look for something more permanent.'

Isabelle once more studied her daughter's reflection, noting with pride that she had inherited her finely-boned physique, her slender, graceful figure and her blonde hair. She failed to acknowledge that Lys's warmth of character came straight from Gilles Dupont, her first husband, who had eventually given up trying to draw out some reciprocal warmth from his wife and had set off in a sea-going yacht to sail the seven seas.

That was three and a half years ago, just before Lys had left the sanctuary of her home for the student-life on the southern bank of the Seine in Paris. Neither Lys nor her mother had seen him since, although he sent a postcard from almost every port . . . to Lys, not her mother . . . and had agreed to Isabelle's demand for a divorce in a similar fashion. Isabelle had lost no time in marrying Oscar Cornaille, a well-known city-banker of infinitive wealth and a veneer of charm.

'Anyway,' Lys went on, not being one to give up easily. 'I don't know why you are objecting. You're going to St. Tropez with Oscar, aren't you? I don't want to stay here on my own. No-one stays in Paris in the summer!'

Isabelle's eyebrows drew together halfway through Lys's reply, although she waited frowning until Lys paused.

'I do wish you would call Oscar, 'Papa', as he has asked you, Lysette, dear! You know, if only you'd soften your attitude towards him, he would open any doors you could wish for, and more besides.

'Indeed, I must tell you, Lysette, Oscar wants you to go into the bank with him. He says he has just the opening for you and he will clear the way with the board. You're a bright girl! You'll soon pick up the procedures. After all, a degree is a degree, no matter what subject you read. No-one need know it was only in business studies!'

Lys glared at her mother.

'Then tell Oscar, 'Thanks, but no thanks!' I don't want to go into banking, Maman. If that was my intention, I would have read mathematics!'

'Then what do you intend to do, now that you've graduated? I'm not having you lie in the sun at St. Tropez, reminding everyone that I am old enough to have a daughter of twenty-one!'

The shrill call of the telephone brought to a close Isabelle's tirade and, with an impatient sigh, she crossed the room and picked up the receiver.

'Yes! Who is this? Oh, I see! Well, no, it's not convenient! I'm afraid it's no concern of mine. I am no longer married to his son. You will have to find someone else to act as his nursemaid! Good-bye!'

She dropped the receiver into its place.

'Really! I don't know what the woman was thinking of! Would I go to stay with Gilles' father to nurse him back to health? Me ... on that backwater of an island! How preposterous!'

'What is the matter with Grandpère?' Lys asked anxiously.

'How should I know? Something about him not being well and worrying about his mill or some such nonsense. I told her, it's no concern of mine! Now, where were we? Ah, yes! You must do as Oscar says, Lysette and ... '

'You can't just dismiss Grandpère like that, Maman! He lives on his own! He must need you or he wouldn't have asked someone to telephone!'

'What the old man needs is someone to take that tumbledown mill off his hands and put him in some sort of home for the elderly. It is Gilles' responsibility, not mine! Etienne Dupont has no claim on me.'

She noticed the quickening of interest on Lys's face. Her eyes narrowed sharply. 'Nor on you, Lysette! I absolutely forbid it!'

Lys was unmoved by her mother's

protestations. She had been forbidden to go to Provence with Danielle, she didn't want to spend the summer being inducted into banking, and she didn't want to spend the summer on her own in their apartment in Paris. Here was her answer!

She would go to Ile d'Oléron, an island off the west coast of Charente Maritime and she would spend the summer there, doing what she could for her grandfather and, no doubt, have time to enjoy herself as well.

None of Isabelle's objections and pleas made any inroad on Lys's decision to help her grandfather and to prove that she could look after herself, and Oscar, when informed on Lysette's decision by his wife, merely raised his eyebrows and then shrugged.

'Let the girl do as she wishes, Isabelle. She'll soon find out what is best in life. She has tasted the life of the privileged. It won't take long before she changes her mind and comes begging to be taken back.'

'No chance!' Lys muttered under her breath. She was already remembering the wonderful holidays she had spent on Ile d'Oléron when she was a child, the slow pace of the island, the freedom, the wonderful beaches, the warm sand and the surf.

'How will you get there?' Isabelle asked, tight-lipped but accepting the inevitable.

Lys looked at her in surprise, thinking of the car that Oscar had given her for her twenty-first birthday. Was he going to demand its return? She threw a questioning glance at her step-father, trying to weigh up his expression.

'Go in the car,' he said lightly. 'It's yours. There are no strings attached.'

Maybe she had underestimated him? The car would certainly make getting around the island much easier.

'And I'll continue your allowance until the end of September,' Oscar continued, ignoring Isabelle. 'And, if you need help in any way, if Etienne is in a bad way, don't be too proud to get in touch.'

'Thanks,' Lys said again, abashed at her earlier unworthy thoughts of him.

She left the next morning and, once clear of Paris, the traffic quickly reduced to minimum and she drove south on the A10 autoroute heading for Saintes.

The bright sunshine that had seen her exit from Paris had now given way to a darkened sky and, a few kilometres after leaving the autoroute, just past a village called Balanzac, a jagged fork of lightning split the darkened sky, followed seconds later by an enormous crash of thunder that seemed to shake the road beneath her.

'Wow! That was close!' she said aloud.

She had never seen a thunderbolt hit anything but was more than willing to believe that the noise had heralded some such occurrence. Two thunderclaps later, huge drops of rain began to splash her windscreen and she had only time to switch on the windscreen wipers before the rain was pelting down so hard that her wipers were unable to cope with the amount of water cascading over the windscreen.

The distorted image of a parking sign came within her range of vision and she decided to make use of the lay-by until the downpour had eased. Thankfully, she guided her car into it, drove to near its far end and put on the brake.

As she switched off the engine, the rear passenger-side door was wrenched open and a thoroughly soaked, be-draggled male figure tossed a large dark bundle on to the rear seat. Before she had time to do more than shout, 'Hey!', the door slammed shut and the front passenger door wrenched open. The wet, bedraggled figure flung himself headfirst into the car, flopped on to the seat at her side and thrust forward a wet brown hand.

'Thanks!' he gasped. 'I didn't think anyone would stop in this weather! You must be my guardian angel in disguise!'

He looked at her startled face and

visibly sagged into his seat, embarrassed realisation flooding his face.

'You didn't stop to pick me up, did you? I'm sorry! I'll make myself scarce! Sorry about the wet seat and everything!'

He turned and tugged at the door handle.

'Sorry! My hands are so cold I can't seem to grip it!'

Lys felt her heart rate begin to subside.

'You're all right. Stay for a few minutes until the rain stops! I can't throw you out in this!'

'Are you sure? I'm very grateful.'

He grinned disarmingly. 'I'm not an escaped convict or a serial killer,' he assured her lightly, 'and I'm very sorry I startled you like that. I truly thought you'd seen me and taken pity on me. Did you hear that first clap of thunder? It was overhead! The lightning was fantastic! I must get it down on canvas as soon as I can!' He smilingly tapped his head. 'I've got it stored in here but

10

it'll lose its impact if I store it too long.'

Lys glanced over the back of her seat at the huge bundle now dripping on to the rear seat and floor. It was a large backpack with various other bundles tied to its outer straps. She saw three wooden legs sticking out of the end of the main part of the backpack.

'You're an artist,' she said, more as a statement than a question.

'Yes. Xavier . . . er . . . Piquet.'

He seemed to pause and, when she gave no reaction, he continued, 'Freelance artist of no fixed abode.'

He held out his hand again and, this time, she took it lightly.

'Lys Dupont,' she returned. 'Freelance ex-student . . . with temporary abode with my grandfather on Ile d'Oléron.'

'Really? That's where I'm heading. Honestly!' he added, seeing her incredulous expression. 'I'm renting a studio where I can paint and exhibit my work, a disused fisherman's hut. There's any number of them lying empty along by the port. Artists and

11

sculptors and suchlike hire them as studios for the summer.'

He studied her face, reading her doubtful expression.

'I'll get out, if you like. I don't want to make you feel obliged to give me a lift . . . only, with you going my way, I must admit it would be a great help.'

Lys relaxed. He certainly looked what he said he was. His long dark brown hair was plaited into dreadlocks, held back off his face by a braided band. His skin was bronzed by the weather and his clothes, although soaking wet, were rough but presentable. Most of her former student friends looked much the same . . . except that Xavier Piquet was much more good-looking.

He cocked his head on one side. 'Am I in or out?'

She laughed. 'You can stay,' she agreed. 'I'll take you to Ile d'Oléron. Count yourself lucky, for I wouldn't usually stop for a hitch-hiker.'

The rain was easing and the sky lightening. Lys glanced in her mirror, making sure that the road was clear.

'Fasten your seat belt and we'll be on our way.'

* * *

The remaining time of the journey passed swiftly. The sudden storm had cleared the road of traffic and light-hearted conversation made the kilometres slip away. Xavier was easy to talk to and Lys found herself sharing some of her frustration at her mother's attempts to mould her life into a shape that suited her.

'So, what do you want to do?' he asked, his eyebrows raising a little, giving the impression that he wasn't too impressed by her protestations.

'I'm not sure exactly,' she admitted, flushing under his direct challenge, 'but I want to make my own way in life. I feel I've got the ability to create something. As an artist, you must understand that.'

'Indeed I do,' Xavier agreed. 'As an

artist, I see things with my soul and transmit what I see to the canvas through my brush.' He studied her profile for a moment. 'It costs a high price to remain true to your soul. Somehow, I don't think you are dedicated enough.'

'What do you mean?' she asked sharply. 'Are you saying I will be a failure?'

'No, of course not, but you will need to know what it is you want to do.' He shrugged his shoulders. 'You want to stand on your own feet but you drive an expensive car and I expect some sort of allowance is paid into a bank account each month. Am I correct?'

Lys glanced at him sharply, irritated by his accurate assessment of the allowance being paid into her bank.

'So what?' she snapped. 'A person has to live! And I didn't see you refusing a lift in my 'expensive' car.'

Xavier laughed at her barbed reply. 'True! But an artist has to experience a degree of suffering. Only then will his inner soul burst through the outer shell!' He appraised her face, smiling a little. 'I do not think you will wish to suffer for your destiny.'

'Well, I suppose you know it all! Are you dedicated enough? Are you willing to suffer?' Lys challenged, annoyed at his ready criticism of her.

Xavier shrugged lightly. 'Yes, if need be! My father wanted me to join the family business, or failing that, to be a surveyor. I tried to please him, but in the end, I just couldn't go through with it. It was stifling me and I ducked out before my finals. Papa was furious and more or less threw me out, but I knew I wanted to paint above anything else.'

'Huh! And your 'ducking out' gives you the right to criticise my indecision about what to do with my life.'

They were crossing the three-kilometre-long viaduct that joined Ile d'Oléron to the mainland and Lys wanted to enjoy her first view of the island for over six years. Its low coastal line stretched out both to the left

15

leading to St. Trojan and to the right to Le Château, two of the dozen or so small towns on the island.

The tide was out, revealing a large expanse of sandy flatland. A series of poles in the shallow water indicated the line of the deeper channels and the positions of oyster beds and mussel grounds.

Lys felt annoyed that her expected pleasure at seeing the familiar scene had been ruined.

'Where shall I drop you off?' she asked brusquely.

'Wherever suits you.'

Lys knew he had seen through her reaction to his words. Who did he think he was, criticising her character and motivation? She pulled into a lay-by immediately after the viaduct, knowing it left him a couple of kilometres to walk into Le Château.

'This do?'

'Fine. Thanks for the lift.'

He got out of the car, opened the rear door and hooked out his ungainly backpack and appendages.

'Thanks again. See you sometime.'

She watched as he casually shrugged his large load on to his back and, with a wave of his hand, he set off towards the fork in the road that led to Le Château.

Lys slipped into first gear and, her tyres spinning on the loose gravel, she regained the road and sped past him, her face set straight ahead as if intent on her destination a few kilometres along the main road through the island.

Lys couldn't resist a glance in her rear mirror just before she drove out of sight of Xavier. The young artist had a spring in his step and seemed unperturbed by having to walk into Le Château under his own steam — he probably preferred it, Lys thought darkly. He could give the impression of having trudged all day!

With a rueful grimace and a short laugh, she acknowledged the unworthiness of her uncharitable thought. Was it because his barb had struck home?

17

A picture of Xavier's face flashed in her mind. He had been laughing at her, she knew.

Huh! If she never saw him again, it would be far too soon!

2

Xavier watched the car disappear round the bend in the road and smiled ruefully. He'd hit a raw nerve there, much as Lys might choose to deny it. Not to worry! He might never see her again, though he had to admit she was an attractive young woman. He shrugged the thought away. His summer plans didn't include time off for romance. His time was too precious for that complication.

As he tramped towards the old fortified town of Le Château, his mind was already concentrating on the memory of the heavy dark clouds that had hung low over the flat countryside of Charente Maritime prior to the storm and how the lightning had spectacularly forked through them.

He thought of the colours of the fields, the vibrant greens of early summer, darkened by the overcast sky; the contrasting red glow of the poppies dancing delicately in the breeze. He began to compose his picture, seeing each aspect in his mind's eye, experiencing that deep-seated joy of created urge that would soon explode itself onto his canvas.

He was on the outskirts of the town now. The port lay down a short road to his right. The main road swung round to the left, past some thriving small restaurants and oyster bars; a small boatyard selling ocean-going yachts; a shop selling nautical equipment and clothes; and over one of the many channels that cut through the low-lying land around the island's coast. This was the route he followed.

Xavier came to a halt by the cluster of simple wooden huts that had served many years as local fishermen's work-huts until they had been taken over by a group of artists and sculptors, anticipating with delight the joy of living in one of them, even of painting them. His glance slid over them, coming to rest on the hut on the right just over the bridge — it was to be his home and studio for the next few months!

The end of the blue-painted hut at the road-facing side consisted of a double door that would be opened wide to display the interior of the hut, which was large enough to accommodate his bed-roll at night; a small primus stove suitable for very basic cooking; a folding canvas chair left by the previous tenant; a small wooden cupboard for a few items of food; and a small partitioned area containing a basic toilet and hand basin . . . leaving plenty of space for his easels and stack of canvasses that had yet to be collected from a temporary postal address he had arranged with the agent who had handled his tenancy agreement.

He glanced around with satisfaction. The walls would hold a good number of completed sketches and paintings and he planned to hold sessions when would-be buyers could watch him at work at various stages of his art or sit for their own likeness to be drawn, an exercise that he knew would draw in the customers. The paintings would be realistically priced. He knew his worth, as did his already-satisfied clients.

Xavier introduced himself to the occupant of the neighbouring hut, who willingly agreed to keep an eye on his pack whilst he went to get the keys off his agent and his painting equipment from his collection point, and he was soon unpacked and had allocated space to his few possessions.

He carefully unwrapped three almost-finished canvasses, each portraying a well-known steeplechaser, and settled them on to three easels he had placed near the open end of the hut.

One showed the horse in full flight over a high brush fence. The second painting was of a horse clearing a hurdle, at that heart-stopping moment when the horse's fore hooves were about to touch the turf and the spectators were holding their breath until the rear hooves touched also and the horse regained momentum.

The third canvas was a horse and jockey being led into the winner's enclosure by the proud owner. He knew he had pandered to the owner's vanity in this one. He had less of a paunch and few rolls of fat around his chin and neck, but the horse was perfect in every detail.

Satisfied for the moment, Xavier stuck *sold* tickets on the three canvasses. They had been commissioned by the horses' owners, but would advertise his skill as an artist until he had any new ones ready.

He glanced casually around. There was nothing else he could do here for now . . . and he was hungry. It was time to sample the local cuisine. The appetising aroma of cooking was drifting from the small restaurant on the edge of the quayside and, from the sound of voices, others had the same idea.

Meanwhile, motoring up the island,

Lys marvelled at how quickly all signs of the heavy thunderstorm had passed. The sun was shining more strongly now and a long-hidden flicker of memory surfaced of having been riding a pony when a storm had struck and by the time she had reached her grandfather's home soaked to the skin, the sun was once more cracking the ground.

She had loved her holidays here with her paternal grandparents and regretted not having been since her parents had split up. It hadn't been a deliberate omission on her part; it had simply been more convenient and more enticing to go with her mother and new husband to such places as Cannes and St Tropez. She had missed even her grandmother's funeral since she was in the middle of first-year examinations . . . and her mother hadn't passed on the news until the summer vacation.

Still, she was here now and intended to more than make it up to her grandfather.

Almost before she knew it, she was

on the road to Dolus, a left turn towards Vertbois, round the next bend into Le Deu, and there it was, Grandpère's windmill and single-storey cottage.

The two buildings seemed smaller than she remembered and both had an air of neglect. Some wooden lattes were missing from the conical roof of the windmill; paint was peeling from the cream walls; the wooden sails were in complete disrepair. A flicker of sadness washed over her. Grandmère had always kept everywhere immaculate, with window boxes at the cottage and tubs filled with geraniums and impatiens.

Now, the window boxes were empty and weeds were growing rampantly amongst the rambling roses and tall hollyhocks and the rest of the enclosed land. The ancient well, the only source of water to the property, was also surrounded by an untidy mass of weeds and flowers, though a track of trampled weeds showed that it was still in use.

She pushed her sad thoughts away. Now that she was here, she would soon put things right. A coat of paint; weeding and planting; and maybe the help of a local handyman for the roof.

Switching off the engine, she rolled her head from side to side and eased back her shoulders. Oh, it was good to stretch her muscles. Leaving her belongings where they were, she went towards the door of the cottage that was set a few metres away from the windmill itself. She knocked softly and opened the door.

'Hello? Grandpère? It's Lysette! Are you there?'

She stepped inside the dim interior. The familiarity of it brought a lump to her throat. It was just as she remembered.

The main living room was sparsely furnished with a wooden table, not as well-scrubbed as it had always been in her grandmother's day; four chairs were set around the table.

Before she could take in any more, a

faint voice from an inner room called an enquiry and Lys hurried across to the open doorway. Etienne Dupont was lying in bed, his much shrunken figure propped up on pillows.

'Grandpère!' Lys cried, hastening forward.

'Ah, Lysette! Is it really you?' He struggled to sit up but the effort was too much for him and he sank back against his pillows. 'It's good to see you, my little one! Madame Giraud told me you were coming but I hardly dared to hope it.'

His voice sounded frail but nonetheless held a note of pleasure and his smile was full of welcome. His face was more lined than she remembered and had lost its bronzed weather-beaten tan. He looked older, and frailer, and Lys found her throat tight with emotion. It was difficult to get any further words out. She hugged her grandfather tightly and, when she eventually pulled away, saw that his eyes were as moist as hers. She laughed shakily.

'We're a fine pair, aren't we? We should be laughing, not crying! Oh, I'm so sorry I haven't been to see you for so long.'

Her voice almost broke as she said the words and she wiped further tears away with the back of her hand.

'No matter, child. You are here now, and I'm glad to see you. Madame Giraud will be pleased also.'

He weakly lifted a hand from off the thin bedcover and waved it vaguely in front of him. 'She has done what she can for me but she has neglected her patisserie in doing so ... but could I tell her so? She takes no notice of anything I say. Comes fussing round here four times a day or more. I tell her it's enough to cause a relapse!'

His voice softened. 'Eh, but it's good to see you child!'

'And it's good to see you, Grand-père!' Lys responded. 'Now, what can I do? A cup of coffee? I'll pop the kettle on and bring some things in and we can have a nice little chat.'

Etienne shook his head. 'The fire isn't lit, Lysette. It's been too hot. Madame Giraud fills a jug with water from the well for me.' He gestured towards a jug on the bedside cupboard. 'A glass of water will do me fine. Pour some into that glass and help me to sit up a little.'

Lys did as instructed, pumping up his pillows to make him more comfortable. Water was fine for her too, so she got herself another glass and carried a chair into the bedroom.

As they chatted, Etienne told of his sudden heart attack but hastened to assure Lys that he was well on the mend and as soon as his fool of a doctor gave the word he would be out of his bed and no trouble to anyone.

'You're no trouble, Grandpère. And I can stay all summer, so you've no need to rush things. That is, if it's all right with you,' she added hesitantly.

His face lit with delight. 'More than all right!' he declared.

A knock on the door drew Lys's

attention but before she had risen from her chair, whoever it was had already stepped into the living room.

'Here she comes! She'll have seen you arrive. I knew her nose would lead her over here before you'd had time to take more than a dozen breaths,' Etienne cackled loudly.

'Grandpère!' Lys hissed, shocked at his impolite manners.

'After fifty years of Etienne Dupont, my skin is too thick to hurt, Mademoiselle Lysette!' the visitor responded, standing in the doorway, casting a quizzical glance at the grinning patient. 'It is good to see you, mademoiselle. Do you remember me?'

Lys rose to greet her and they exchanged the traditional French cheek-to-cheek kisses.

'Yes, of course, Madame! And I remember your lovely pastries and croissants. Thank you for the way you have taken care of Grandpère.'

'It's a wonder I'm not dead, the way the woman fusses,' Etienne grumbled.

'Get away with you, you grouchy old man! You've been glad enough to see me coming through that door!'

Madame Giraud was a lady in her late fifties, Lys guessed. Her grey hair was fashioned in a bun at the base of her head and her round face bore a cheerful smile.

'Sit down, Madame Giraud,' Lys invited, indicating her chair.

'Don't bother asking her. She never has time!' Etienne grumbled sourly. 'A fellow could die of boredom round here and not be missed by his neighbour!'

'Grandpère!'

Lys was embarrassed and turned to apologise to their visitor but realised that there was no need. Madame Giraud was standing with her hands on her hips, a ready riposte on her lips.

'I'd miss your grumpiness, all right! I can tell you, mademoiselle, there's not been a worse patient in the whole of Christendom than this old fraud. Had us all thinking he was dying, he did.

31

Just after a bit of attention, if you ask me.'

Lys laughed. She could tell from Madame Giraud's tone of voice that it was all in good humour.

'Aren't all men the same.'

'I was dying!' Etienne protested. 'I just thought I'd stay around a bit longer to plague you all! Besides, I just wanted to see my granddaughter again, and here she is.'

Madame Giraud left the bedroom. When she was at the outer door, she turned and smiled at Lys.

'Take no notice of our bickering! He'd have another heart attack if I was polite to him.'

'How poorly was he really?' Lys asked anxiously.

Madame Giraud's face sobered. 'He had us all worried, I can tell you that. He wanted to see you, and your father, too, of course . . . every father wants to see his son before he dies.'

'I don't know where he is,' Lys faltered. 'Is Grandpère still that poorly?'

'He's doing all right, don't worry. Another week in bed and then an easy few weeks or so and he'll be as right as rain, just you see. Just don't let that Monsieur Fayau in to see him, that's all. It was his last visit that brought all this on, I reckon.'

'Who's Monsieur Fayau?'

'Michel Fayau. A local good-for-nothing old rogue, that's who he is. He wants to buy up all the properties around here but most of us don't want to sell. We've all said no, but he doesn't seem ready to accept defeat yet.'

With a reminder to Lys to collect their supper later, Madame Giraud departed and Lys returned inside. Etienne had fallen asleep. She would ask him about Michel Fayau later, after he had awakened.

She emptied the boot of her car and carried everything inside. The same bed was in the small bedroom. Clean sheets had been laid on top of it and a selection of folded blankets.

She peeped in at Grandpère to make

sure he was all right and then strolled outside into the still-warm air, appreciative of the stillness after the constant buzz of traffic and people in Paris.

Hands on hips, she critically made note of the face-lift that the buildings needed, giving no more than a passing glance to the car that was coming to a stop on the spare ground. She moved closer to the windmill. A bit of the sail crumbled in her hand as she touched it. The two outer doors, on opposite sides of the windmill, weren't in any better condition and slivers of paint from the wall of the circular mill flaked onto her fingers.

'As you can see,' a male voice spoke behind her, 'the whole lot needs to be pulled down.'

3

Lys turned around, finding herself face-to-face with a man of thirty-something, dressed in a suit, collar and tie.

'I beg your pardon,' she said haughtily, not liking the derisive tone of his voice.

'The building is unsafe. It's a danger to the public and ought to be demolished.'

'And you are . . . '

'Leon Boudot, mademoiselle.'

He held out his hand. 'I am a borough surveyor and have been asked to give my opinion about the safety of this building to the local housing department. I am here to make a preliminary survey and advise my colleagues about what steps need to be taken to re-house Monsieur Dupont. There is some concern about Monsieur

Dupont's capability of looking after himself.'

Lys had taken hold of his hand but dropped it as if burned as he continued to speak and took a step backwards.

'Re-house my grandfather? Are you mad? It would kill him if he had to leave here! There must be some mistake!'

She waved her hand towards the windmill and cottage. 'The buildings aren't that bad. I know they need some work doing on them, but there's no way they need to be pulled down.'

'That is what I am here to determine, mademoiselle. And you are ... ?' Monsieur Boudot imitated Lys's own earlier question, his eyebrow raised quizzically.

Lys drew herself to full height. 'I am Lysette Dupont, Etienne Dupont's granddaughter, and there is no way that I am going to let you into either the windmill or the cottage so that you can certify them as uninhabitable.'

'You will have no choice, mademoiselle. Although I have no written authority today, it will only be a formality to obtain such documentation. It would be advisable to grant me access today before the matter is official. You never know, I may be able to make some suggestions for renovations before the official visit takes place. Let's start with the windmill, shall we?'

Lys stood her ground. Something, she didn't quite know what, made her distrust the man.

'May I see your identification card, monsieur?'

Boudot smirked openly.

'But of course, mademoiselle!'

He reached into the inner pocket of his jacket and pulled out a slim, folded card, which he flicked open in front of Lys.

Lys glanced at the card and sniffed dismissively. 'I still can't help you. I have only arrived this afternoon and I don't know where my grandfather keeps his keys. He is fast asleep and needs his rest. I have no intention of disturbing him.'

The man's eyes narrowed slightly. 'You will be well advised, mademoiselle, to encourage your grandfather to sell his property whilst he can, before a demolition order is placed on it. That would deter prospective buyers, believe me.'

Lys followed his glance towards the windmill, trying to look at it objectively. It was nearly two hundred years old and had already withstood many a winter storm. She was certain it wasn't as bad as this man would have her believe. Hands on her hips, she faced him squarely.

'I'll advise my grandfather to get a surveyor of his own,' she said curtly. 'Now, if you will be so good as to leave our land, I can get on with my work.'

Reluctant to accept defeat so easily, the man hesitated, but Lys refused to give way. She didn't like him, and didn't trust him. The sooner she was rid of him, the better.

Boudot abruptly turned on his heel and strode back to his car. With a squeal of his tyres on the loose chippings, he roared away.

Grandpère's voice greeted her return to the cottage. 'Lysette! Come here, girl!'

'I'm here, Grandpère! What is it?'

'I heard voices. Who is it? It's not that Michel Fayau, is it? Don't let him in here. I'll have nothing to do with him. He's a scoundrel. A rogue! I wouldn't trust him to blow on my coffee without drinking half of it!'

'It's all right! It wasn't Fayau. It was a man called Leon Boudot, a local surveyor.' She briefly explained the purpose of his visit but laid a hand on her grandfather's arm when she saw signs of his agitation. 'Don't worry, Grandpère. I wouldn't let him in and he's gone. Now, don't worry about it. No-one can make you do anything you don't want to. Even if you can't work the windmill, you can still live here.'

She glanced round the dim interior,

shuddering slightly at the thought of living for more than a few weeks in its austerity, especially if she were still here next winter. No electricity, no plumbed-in water, and a well in the courtyard. Was it really a suitable place for an old man?

Memory of Leon Boudot's smirking face gave her a determination she didn't know she had. She would make sure the place was suitable for him.

'I'd like to look around the windmill, Grandpère, before the light goes. Where's the key?'

'It's on the hook by the door. Take care, Lys. There's not much light in there and I've not been inside for a few weeks.'

She took the key and went outside to the windmill, going to the nearest door. The heavy key grated in the lock but an extra twist released the mechanism and she pushed the door open.

It was quite dark inside since the windows were tiny and needed a good clean. The floor was composed of stone flags on packed earth and, although dusty, needed no more than a good sweep out. She knew it hadn't been used as a corn windmill for many years, but all of the old equipment was still in various stages of disrepair, covered in layers of dust.

Large empty flour sacks lay piled on a bench near the long wooden chute that came down from the floor above. She stepped nearer and tentatively fingered a cobweb.

Grandpère had lost heart after Grandmère had died. She'd heard it said but hadn't really taken in what it meant. It was obvious to her now that he had just lost all interest in his work.

Tears pricked her eyes but she shook them away. It was no use crying over the past. What she needed to do now was to think of a way to inspire him to work again.

Oh, not in the windmill. He wouldn't be strong enough to cope with that, but there was no reason why he couldn't make his home a bit smarter, maybe

41

have electricity installed and water pumped in. Life would be a bit easier for him, then.

She looked dubiously at the flight of wooden steps that curved around the inner edge of the wall, leading up to the next floor, wondering if it were safe to climb up. She grasped the side of the handrail firmly and tried to shake it. It stood firm. Treading carefully, she ascended slowly.

This section housed the chute that directed the milled grains from the millstones into the series of sieves that separated the ground corn into three grades. Remembering the rigorous movement of the drums that held the sieves, she doubted that they would be strong enough to perform the necessary action.

Pursing her lips thoughtfully, she looked at the next flight of steps. The flight was narrower and the handrail moved slightly when she shook it. The light was poorer, too. When the windmill was working, a hatch would be open, allowing the sacks of corn to be hauled inside for the hoist and pulley system, but that was fastened shut. She went as far as three steps from the top and looked around.

She glanced around. As far as she could determine, the general structure of the windmill was sound, but she would do as she had said to Leon Boudot. She would get a surveyor to come and give them an independent opinion . . . and keep Grandpère's home intact.

Realising that she could do nothing else tonight, she descended carefully and locked the door behind her.

Grandpère was dozing comfortably and she made a quick inspection of the store cupboard. There were some tins of meat, fish, soup and vegetables; a pot of butter; half a pot of jam and some biscuits.

Madame Giraud had been providing meals for Grandpère but she couldn't let her go on doing so now that she was here. The woman had enough to do to keep her patisserie well-stocked. She had a mental vision of her younger self gazing through the patisserie window and being allowed to choose her favourite pastry from its tantalising mouth-watering display.

She smiled at the memory, conscious that the food was making her feel hungry. If she hurried, she would be in time to get some bread and pastries for their meal and so she strolled along the road towards the tiny village of Le Deu.

The grocer's shop was no longer there, though window boxes and tubs filled with bright flowers showed that the house was still lived in.

The patisserie was closed. Lys knocked and stepped inside.

Madame Giraud came through from the back.

'Ah! Come in. come in, Lysette. Has Etienne sent you for your dinner? I am just about to serve it out. It's a fish pie today. Etienne's favourite!'

She turned and bustled back into the kitchen. Lys followed her, sniffing

44

appreciatively at the aroma of cooking and freshly-baked bread.

'Grandpère's asleep. He didn't say you were making our meal, but it's very kind of you, Madame Giraud. I'll have a lot to live up to, now that I'm here to look after Grandpère instead of you.' She laughed depreciatively at herself. 'I'm no cook to speak of, I'm afraid.'

Madame Giraud shrugged. 'It's no hardship for me to continue, Lysette. Cooking for one, two, three, it is no different. It takes no longer. Etienne pays his way, you know.'

'Oh?'

She hadn't known, though she should have, she realised. Grandpère had his pride.

'But your patisserie? Your time?'

Madame Giraud gave a hollow laugh. 'I bake a few loaves, a few baguettes, flutes and such, some croissants for breakfast and pastries for afternoon tea, but business is slack.'

She sighed heavily. 'It's the super-markets, you see. They can do it all so much more cheaply than I can. They have more variety for less money. What are people to do? I cannot blame them for taking their custom there. They buy all they need in one shop. Maybe we should do as Michel Fayau wants and sell out to him?'

'Why does he want your properties? He must have something in mind. He wouldn't risk making a loss.'

Madame Giraud shook her head. 'We don't know. He must know something! He has friends on the council. Someone must have leaked something to him, but no-one is saying.'

'Someone like Leon Boudot?' Lys suggested.

'Very probably. Why do you mention him?'

Lys explained about his visit, and her decision to get an independent survey.

'It will cost money. And how will you get one whom you can trust?'

'I don't know. I'll have to think about it. Anyway, I mustn't keep you. Thank

you for the casserole. It smells deli-
cious.'

Lys returned to the windmill cottage
deep in thought, trying to think of a
solution to her grandfather's problems.
There was one option she could take!

★   ★   ★

The following day, before Lys had done
no more than collect some croissants
from the patisserie, drawn water from
the well and made a pot of coffee, she
heard a car drawing up outside. A
glance through the window showed it to
be Leon Boudot again.

'Can't you even let people have their
breakfast in peace?' she demanded, not
pausing to make the customary greet-
ing.

'It is after nine o'clock,' Boudot said
smoothly.

She relaxed her stance. He had
warned her he would be coming back.
She just hadn't expected him this early.
She was glad she'd had time to look at

47

the windmill the previous evening. At least she knew it wasn't in too bad a state.

'Anyway, you'll have to wait until I've cleared away my grandfather's tray. I can't leave it on his knees. He might knock it off if he falls asleep.'

'If you'd only see sense and get him in a nursing home or something, you wouldn't need to be acting as nurse-maid to him.'

If Boudot thought his reasonable tone of voice would win him any points, he was sadly mistaken. Lys was incensed by his words.

'How dare you tell me or my grandfather what to do? It's none of your business! You are supposed to be giving us an authorised assessment of the safety of our property. I think you had better keep to your remit.'

Boudot eyed speculatively and snapped into official mode.

'Right, Mademoiselle Dupont. As soon as you are ready, I am here at your disposal. I will wait in my car.'

Lys watched as he strode back to his car and re-seated himself inside it. She was unperturbed at ruffling his feathers. His attitude had annoyed her and she felt sure that he had no official backing to speak as he had.

She went back into the cottage and told her grandfather that Boudot had arrived and was going to assess the condition of the windmill.

'But the structure is quite sound, I'm sure,' she assured him. 'It only needs some running repairs and a lick of paint.'

'But what's the use?' Grandpère sighed dispiritedly. 'I'm too old. I just want to be left in peace.'

'If it keeps the authorities happy, we'll do everything we can to make sure it's safe and then there'll be no need to sell the windmill or have it pulled down. I can run up a ladder and do some painting and I can't wait to get rid of all those weeds out there. We'll soon have it looking like it used to.'

Etienne didn't look convinced but

Lys felt enthusiastic about restoring the exterior of the windmill and cottage to its former prettiness, and hoped she could also persuade her grandfather to modernise his cottage a bit.

Within five minutes, she went outside and approached Boudot's car. Another man was with him, she saw. They both got out and Boudot nodded briefly towards his companion.

'My clerk,' he said briefly. 'Show Mademoiselle Dupont our authorisation. She likes to go by the book.'

His companion drew out a paper and held it out for Lys to read. She took it from him and skim-read it. It seemed to be in order. She folded it up and slipped it into the rear pocket of her jeans.

'I'll read it in detail later.'

She took the key for the windmill from another pocket and led the way over to the windmill and opened the door.

'It's a bit dusty in here,' she said over her shoulder, 'but I think you'll find everything quite sound. This floor is flagged and . . . '

'I would prefer it if you let me make my own assessment, mademoiselle,' Boudot said coolly, pausing in the doorway to poke at the wooden doorframe.

'Well-rotted,' he murmured, nodding at his clerk, who dutifully wrote it down, 'and the door needs to be replaced, as well. The other's probably just as bad, so make that two doors and frames.'

He took a metal rod out of his pocket and scraped along where the walls joined the floor.

'Crumbling walls,' he said shortly. 'They need to be re-pointed and resurfaced.'

He stood in the centre of the ground floor and glanced around pursing his lips. Finding nothing else to comment on there, he strode over to the staircase, shook it slightly and then climbed up it. Lys made as if to follow but the man made her stay on the ground floor. 'You stay as well!' he commanded his clerk. 'I'll call details down to you.'

She could hear him striding about on the next floor, then a thud as if he had jumped to test its strength. A short silence followed and she imagined him poking at the floorboards or into the walls. The silence lengthened and Lys began to feel apprehensive. What was he doing?

'The next staircase is weak,' he called down. 'I'm about to test it for weight-bearing.'

'No, it's not!' Lys objected, taking a step towards the wooden staircase. Before she reached it a shout echoed above, followed by a crash.

She froze. What had happened?

She exchanged a glance with the clerk and they both moved towards the steps at the same instant. Lys got there first. Careless of her own safety, she ran up the steps. Boudot was half-sitting, half-lying at the foot of the next staircase, except, as her eyes adjusted to the dimmer light, she realised that the handrail to the staircase was no longer there. It lay at her feet in broken pieces.

Boudot was dazedly pushing himself to his knees and struggling to his feet.

'I think we have the answer as to the soundness of the windmill, mademoiselle. Don't you? In my opinion, it would be best to pull it down before it falls down.'

4

Xavier had wakened early that morning and was instantly alert. Ten minutes later, he was seated at the end of the pier munching an apple as he watched the sky change colour with the rising sun.

The intrusive putt-putt of an engine drew his gaze towards the main channel that flowed straight out of the port towards Bourcefranc on the mainland. He swiftly flipped open his sketchpad and drew a quick outline-drawing of the flat-bottomed boat that was setting out to visit the oyster beds in the deeper water that flowed between the island and the mainland.

Deep-sea fishing and the culture of oysters and mussels were two of the mainstay industries of the island. There'd be the farming community as well, the melon growers and vintners, the market traders and . . .

The image of a windmill flitted into his inner vision and he thought of his encounter with Lys, who was going to stay with her grandfather, a former miller, that was another ancient trade of the island.

He vaguely stored the idea in a corner of his mind as he got to his feet.

There would be other activities in the port to sketch if he made his way back along the quayside.

Later, he bought a couple of croissants from a café in the main square and returned to his hut, where he spent the morning setting up his simple studio.

Deciding to break for lunch, he left his work on display and sauntered along to the small restaurant beyond the road bridge where he ordered a grilled fillet of sole and a glass of wine.

It was too hot in the afternoon to set off reconnoitring any more of the local scenery, so Xavier decided to knock together a few simple easels and prepare some canvasses in the cool interior of his hut and go exploring later.

Engrossed in his task, he was suddenly aware that someone had entered his hut and was silently watching him, and he was surprised to see that it was his chauffeuse of the previous day. He was startled by the pleasure that coursed around his body.

'Salut!' he greeted her.

'Salut!'

Lys glanced around. 'It hasn't taken you long to get started,' she said casually.

Xavier grinned. 'I told you, I am dedicated to my work!'

'Hmm! What are you doing?'

'Preparing some canvasses. This cloth, it's called 'duck', has to be stretched on to a frame and then primed with gesso. I usually put three coats on to get a good finish, and then I have to let it dry.'

'Why are you doing three at once?'

'Because I usually like to work on at least three paintings at any one time unless I am doing something that really grips me.'

He eyed her quizzically, wondering why she had searched him out. He hadn't expected her to, but he was pleased that she had, even though she obviously wasn't ready to disclose her reason as she had stepped away from him and was studying the three equine paintings by the door.

'They're good!' she finally declared, with a note of surprise in her voice. 'How do you come to know horses so well?'

'I . . . er . . . used to work in a stable where horses are trained for steeple-chasing and show jumping. I . . . keep in touch every so often.'

'Doesn't painting for money upset your principle of painting your 'soul'?' she asked mischievously.

Xavier grinned, acknowledging her insight. 'The money I earn from commissions allows me to indulge myself in painting from my soul. Even artists have to live. I am fortunate that I am able to do both.'

Lys looked at him hesitantly. 'Would you be willing to do . . . other things for money?'

He raised an eyebrow. 'Other things? What sort of 'other things'?'

She shrugged slightly, as if reluctant to say what she had in mind, and then said diffidently. 'Like a bit of survey- ing?'

She paused, and then hurried on, 'You did say you had nearly qualified. I'm sure you must have covered most of your course, even though you ducked out before your exams. We wouldn't expect it to be perfect, just a general idea, something to go on.'

'And what do you need me to survey? As you say, I couldn't give you a certified opinion, and you wouldn't have any legal right to quote my assessment or anything.'

'Oh, I know. That doesn't matter. We can't really afford to pay a proper surveyor, you see, not without borrowing the money from my step-father, and we don't really want to do that.'

'But you don't mind asking an unqualified stranger?'

Her cheeks reddened. 'We don't expect you to do it for nothing. We'll pay whatever you think is a fair price.'

'Are those your own scruples or your grandfather's?'

'There's no need to be so hateful. Grandpère doesn't know I'm asking you, as it happens. He probably wouldn't like it, but I don't know what else to do.'

She stopped abruptly and her shoulders sagged as she began to turn away. 'It doesn't matter. Forget I asked.'

Xavier's voice softened. 'Come back. I'm teasing you! Why don't you explain what it's all about and then I can say what I think about it? Come on, I owe you anyway for the lift.'

Lys shrugged and stepped nearer again. 'OK. It's about Grandpère's windmill.'

She explained what had happened . . . Michel Fayau's visit, Leon Boudot's first visit, her own quick tour of inspection, Boudot's return earlier that day, and his assessment of the crumbling masonry and the collapse of part of the upper staircase.

'But I know it wasn't that bad. I went up it.'

'But very warily, I presume?'

'That was only because it was dark up there. I felt quite safe.'

'Why didn't you go up with him this morning?'

'He told me not to . . . and his clerk.'

She remembered the few minutes when she was wondering what he was doing.

'I reckon he did a bit of loosening work up there.'

Xavier swivelled round on his stool to face her. 'Why would he do that? Surely, if he works for the local authority, he should have no personal interest in the matter?'

'He shouldn't have. But he wouldn't be the first to have a hand in someone's pocket. Besides, he did sort of threaten me.'

She tried to remember the exact words Boudot had said. 'Something like being advised to sell before a demolition order was placed on it.'

'That doesn't sound very threatening.'

'It was the way he said it. And he had already made up his mind that it was in need of demolition!'

Lys could see her only chance of a reasonably priced survey slipped out of her grasp. 'Please, Xavier! Just ten minutes or so will be enough!'

Xavier laughed. 'I see how poorly you rate my capabilities, Lys!'

Lys turned to go but Xavier called her back.

'OK! OK! I tell you what, persuade your grandfather to sit for me and I'll do it for nothing. What d'you say about that? Fair deal?'

'Why should you want to paint Grandpère? You don't know what he looks like.'

Xavier grinned. 'If he's anything like his granddaughter, he'll be a stubborn old soul with his character written all over his face. I'm thinking of doing a series on local industries and the people who work in them. It's just an idea.'

He turned back to the canvas he was preparing, as if he had lost interest. Lys had to make up her mind quickly.

'All right,' she said. 'It's a deal, as long as you're sure you can afford to do it for free.'

'I sold two sketches this morning,' he said lightly. 'I have a good pitch here. Who knows, I might be a millionaire by the end of the season.'

Lys relaxed and returned his smile. 'I hope so! Maybe I'd better buy one of your paintings now, whilst I can still afford it. When can you come?'

'I'll come as soon as I've prepared these three canvasses. They'll need to set before I work on them anyway. Are you in your car?'

'No. I've just bought a second-hand bicycle from the bike shop. It'll save on petrol money, part of my character building.'

Xavier laughed. 'Touché! Actually, I could do with one myself for getting around the island. So that's another debt I owe you . . . introduce me to your bicycle shop and I'll get a rusty old bike for a song.'

'Or a sketch?'

'Who knows?'

When he had done all he could for the time being, Xavier closed his hut, locked the double doors and walked the short distance to Rue Marechal Foch with Lys.

He purchased a bicycle in reasonable condition for cash and they set off through the country lanes, through Ors and La Chevalerie and on to a cycle path that took them most of the way back to the windmill.

The windmill, when they reached it, was everything Xavier wished for. Even in its neglected state, it had character. He instinctively knew that it was to be a good subject for painting and sketching. Having heard Lys's plans for its face-lift, he was glad to have seen it first in its state of neglect. It blended in with unkempt surroundings and he knew he would paint as such as often as he would in its renovated condition, if it proved sound enough to be renovated.

Lys took him into the cottage to meet her grandfather. He drew in his breath, causing Lys to look at him sharply.

'What's the matter?'

'Nothing. It's wonderful. I bet this cottage has looked like this for over a hundred years. You must keep it as it is. It's marvellous!'

'Yes, except when you have to live in it. There's no electricity or running water and is freezing in wintertime.'

'Yes, but think of the history here. You're going to have to restore it very sensitively. Cottages like this must be a rarity. People would flock to see it.'

'There are a few around. There's one at Le Grand Village. It's a sort of museum, a farm and ancient farming equipment. A folk group called Les

Dejhouqués look after it. You must go and see it one day. Anyway, come through and meet Grandpère, and then I'll take you to see the windmill at close quarters. I'll just make sure he's awake.'

Xavier heard a frail voice declare, 'Of course I'm awake, girl! How do you expect me to sleep with all that racket?' but he gathered from Lys's reply that the grouchiness was a front.

He followed her into the dim bedroom and shook Etienne's thin hand.

'I'm delighted to meet you, Monsieur Dupont. What an interesting home you have. It makes my fingers itch to start painting it.'

'Can't afford any decorators,' Etienne stated firmly. 'Lys tells me she'll do what's needed. Anyway, it isn't worth it. Condemned it is.'

'How do you know that, Grandpère?' Lys asked in surprise. 'I didn't tell you because I didn't want to upset you.'

'Boudot came back after you'd gone. He said he could claim compensation

65

for his injuries, but he won't, if I agree to sell the land to someone who is prepared to develop it, and we know who that will be, don't we!'

'Michel Fayau, I suppose.'

'You haven't agreed, have you?' Xavier asked quickly.

'Sort of. He didn't give me much option. I can't afford to pay compensation, that's for sure.'

'He had no right to put pressure on you like that,' Xavier said firmly. 'You didn't sign anything, did you?'

'No. He said he'll be back on Monday, no, Tuesday. It's the Pentecost holiday this weekend, isn't it?'

'It is indeed. That gives us three days to look into it. I'll get on with the survey, shall I?'

'It's no use throwing good money after bad,' Etienne said wearily. 'I've just got to accept it. My home is done for. I'm sorry, Lysette. I know you wanted to make it look nice for me, but I've left it too late.'

The catch in his voice made Lys take

hold of his hand.

'It mightn't be, Grandpère. Xavier trained as a surveyor. He's going to give us a second opinion.'

* ★ *

Xavier spent the next two hours going through the windmill, poking into the walls and floorboards, testing the first stairway and examining the fallen pieces of the second one.

Xavier looked down at the notes he had made.

'There is quite a bit of woodwork that needs to be renewed in order to make it absolutely safe, but the stonework is very sound. It just needs some pointing and the rendering renewed. The sails are well rotted, of course, and would need to be replaced, and much of the roof needs to be repaired.

'I've not examined the state of the machinery up in the roof space. The parts I've seen seem to be in need of some repair or replacement but that doesn't affect the state of the structure of the building.'

'But, what's the point of repairing it?' Etienne asked despairingly. 'Even if I could afford it, I can't run it commercially. The government put a stop to that, years ago! The large companies would undercut me, for another thing. And I'm too old, and my state of health . . . '

His voice trailed away and he sank back against the pillows.

Lys squeezed his hand. 'I think I know what's in Xavier's mind, Grand-père. He's thinking of us operating it as a sort of 'living museum'.'

She looked eagerly at Xavier. 'Am I right? Like I was telling you about the old farm at Le Grand Village? Only, we'll be actually working it and still producing flour, even if it is in small amounts.'

Xavier nodded. 'Yes. And I think you would qualify for a grant of some sort towards its restoration. I know someone who will be able to advise you properly. Shall I get in touch with her on your behalf? If she's available, I'm sure, as a favour to me, she'll come down to have a look. What do you say?'

Lys's eyes sparkled with enthusiasm. 'Oh, yes!'

She turned excitedly to her grandfather. 'We could get it working again, Grandpère. And people would pay to come in to see it and maybe buy some of the flour we produce! It wouldn't be like full-time, just an hour or so each day, and you could teach me how to do it. I'm sure I'd be up to it.'

Etienne shook his head sadly. 'But you're forgetting Leon Boudot, both of you. If I don't sell, he'll lay charges of injury through negligence against me. I'll be in debt for the rest of my life.'

'I'm not too certain about that,' Xavier said, holding out a length of wood for them to see. 'This is the piece from the top of the broken handrail. It's my belief that it didn't just give way. It had been deliberately loosened and the brackets removed, and very recently, too, I would say.' He looked at Lys. 'You said you went up the staircase yesterday, didn't you?'

Lys nodded.

'Well, if this bracket had been removed before that, the rail wouldn't have held your weight. You would have been the one to fall. It's my belief that Leon Boudot deliberately caused his own accident, and I reckon this bracket proves it.'

Faced with the evidence in his hands, Lys lent him her mobile phone and Xavier went outside to phone his friend, while Lys went over her rapidly expanding hopes for the windmill's future.

Xavier, too, felt enthusiastic about the project. He felt a strong attraction towards Lys, something that had started the previous day, even though their meeting had been less than promising.

He shook his head. Although the thought was pleasant, it wasn't the right time. He needed to work hard during his stay on the island. Pushing the pleasant thoughts away, he turned to the task in hand and dialled Jocelyn's number. He knew she was on holiday with some friends on Ile de Ré, a small island about a hundred kilometres away to the north of La Rochelle, from where she had planned to visit him for a day during her holiday.

The phone crackled to life and he spent a few moments in light-hearted chit-chat before briefly explaining the situation to her.

Lys had stayed just inside the cottage to give Xavier privacy in his call, wondering if this Jocelyn were more than just a friend. Now that the call was over, she sauntered outside, realising from Xavier's pleased expression that his friend had agreed to come.

'She'll probably stay overnight,' he said casually, 'so can you recommend a good hotel? My own illustrious accommodation won't be quite to her taste.'

Lys felt suddenly jealous of the

unknown Jocelyn.

'There's the Hôtel de France, just off the main square, and a few others. They might be booked up for the weekend, though. Oh, and they might want a deposit. Can you, er . . . ? That is . . . '
She felt embarrassed for him. He probably hadn't enough money to pay up front. 'I can lend you some from my allowance, if you need it.'

It suddenly occurred to her that Jocelyn was coming to help her grandfather.

'Or maybe we should be paying the whole amount?'

Xavier held up his hand. 'Don't worry about it. Jocelyn was coming anyway. Besides,' he grinned, 'I can always promise to paint a picture of the hotel to pay the bill.'

Lys laughed. 'By the time you're famous, that many people will have one of your paintings, there'll be no-one left to buy any.'

Her face was full of vitality and Xavier felt a sudden lurch deep inside him, longing to capture her expression on canvas. He would paint her, one day soon. For now, he just laughed and said he must be going.

'I'll ride home by the coast,' he said. 'I need to reconnoitre the area. Lock up the windmill and don't let anyone go inside until Jocelyn has seen everything.'

Xavier took his time meandering through the local lanes. There were many attractive cottages, picturesque gardens, wild, unkempt sand dunes and the long sandy beach.

Every so often, he stopped and took his sketch-pad out of his backpack, swiftly sketching his ideas, some as working drawings, others complete as they were. He had an instinctive eye for what would sell easily.

When he got back to the hut, he leaned up his bike against the side and fumbled in his pocket for the key to the door. Some instinct made him touch the door, and it began to swing outwards towards him. The light was dim but he could see that his belongings had been thrown all over the place.

The faint sound of a footstep behind him made him half-turn but, before he could see who it was, a firm shove in the centre of his back sent him sprawling into his hut.

5

Xavier crashed to the floor. He felt as though all his breath had been knocked out of his body and couldn't have moved had his life depended upon it, which it very well might, he thought desperately as two strong hands hauled his body a half-metre from the ground before slamming him down again.

He groaned as his chest hit the ground, thankful that it was a wooden floor and not stone flags.

He was now being kicked viciously in his ribs. He curled himself inwards, as tightly as he could, to protect his abdomen and ribs. The action left his back exposed.

He sensed that there were three men attacking him. One of the men picked his head off the ground and slammed it back down again.

'What have you done with it?' the man snarled.

Another kick in the lower part of his back jerked his body.

Done with it? Done with what?

His head was raised and slammed down again.

'Where is it?' the same harsh tones demanded.

Xavier's thoughts scattered and disappeared. He felt mindless and wanted only for the violence to end. He couldn't make any sounds, he couldn't see. He drifted into darkness, and release from pain.

* * *

It was completely dark when he came round. At first he couldn't move. Each time he flexed a muscle, pain screamed through his body. With another groan, he dropped back to the ground.

What had they wanted? 'Where is it? What have you done with it?' Where was what, for heaven's sake?

He realised that his body was shaking. He was cold. He hoped they had left him his sleeping bag. Could he manage to crawl over to the back of the hut? Slowly, he rolled himself on to his knees, trying to ignore the pain, and crept slowly to where he hoped the rear of the hut was. If his sleeping bag weren't there, he would just have to curl into a ball and hope to sleep.

He could feel tubes of paint under his knees, and brushes, lengths of wood, which he presumed were his easels broken in pieces. He pushed them aside. Time to think of those tomorrow.

A few minutes of tentatively reaching out his hand to detect the material of his sleeping bag eventually paid off. He dragged it towards him, managed to find the open end and painfully wriggled himself into it.

Then, he slept.

He had no idea what time it was when he awoke. It must have been well into the morning because the small patches of sky he could see through his windows were bright blue. Then his mind erupted into clarity and he slowly pushed himself into a sitting position and looked around his hut. It was a shambles.

His sketches had been torn from the walls and screwed into unrecognisable rubbish, his equipment had been trashed, and the contents of his backpack strewn around the floor. Whatever it was they thought he had must have been worth the trouble, and they had done their best to find it. Would they be satisfied that he hadn't got it? Or would they be back to try more persuasion?

He couldn't be sure. At least they would find him on his feet and not so easy a push-over. He painfully pulled himself out of his sleeping bag and struggled to his feet. Leaning one hand against the wall of the hut, he staggered to the tiny washbasin and did his best to spruce himself up.

He hobbled into the main area and

looked among the debris. There was no sign of them. They had stolen his three horse paintings. Were they what they were after?

No, they couldn't be. They'd said 'it'. 'What have you done with it?' They had already trashed his hut before he came home. He remembered seeing a glimpse of the interior before he had been pushed to the ground.

He gave up. Whatever it was, he hadn't got it, not now and not then. They'd got the wrong guy.

He needed a mug of strong, black coffee. He had no alternative but to face the outside world and hope he didn't look as bad as he felt.

'Wow! What does the other fellow look like?' Paul, the owner of the restaurant along the road, greeted him.

'A lot better than me!' Xavier mumbled through puffed lips. 'I think there were three of them. They jumped me! Can I have a coffee? Strong, black and loads of sugar.'

Paul listened sympathetically to his

tale, shaking his head. 'Are you going to report it to the police?'

Xavier nodded . . . if only for his paintings. They'd be easily recognisable by anyone in the art world if they were ever put on display.

On his return to his hut, Xavier caught sight of his reflection in a shop window. What a mess. He called in a pharmacy for some painkillers.

Jocelyn was arriving around noon and he had promised to meet her outside his hut.

'Which wall did you walk into?'

'Not a wall! It was the floor, and three thugs.'

She was immaculately attired in a cool-looking, cream linen suit and cream strappy sandals. Her fair curls were tied back with a scarlet chiffon scarf, the exact shade of the lipstick she wore.

She raised her eyebrow at the state of his temporary home but knew Xavier well enough to know that he preferred a simple existence when he was painting, and his chameleon-like ability to blend into the very heart of whatever community he was desirous of painting enabled him to soak up the local ambience and give his work authenticity.

Even so . . .

'This is a bit basic, even for you, Xavier.'

Xavier grinned. 'What more do I need?'

'A bit of pampering, from the look of you. Let me at least book you into a hotel whilst I'm here. I can stay until Monday evening if you wish.'

Xavier shook his head. 'No. I've already made friends here and they accept me as I am. Come on, let's have some lunch, whilst I tell you in more detail what it's all about.'

They ordered a light lunch and, whilst they ate it, Xavier explained as much as he knew about the situation at the windmill.

'And what if I disagree with your opinion?'

'Then, nothing. They will still have the option to apply for a grant towards restoration, but they may have legal bills to pay out to this Leon Boudot. That would probably be the end of the matter. They would have to sell and move elsewhere, which would be a pity.'

'And you would have to look elsewhere for some models. Is she pretty?'

He painfully grinned self-consciously at his sister's perception. 'Who?'

'The miller's granddaughter!'

He tried to look indifferent but a slight reddening of his swollen cheeks betrayed that he did have an underlying motive.

'I just don't like to see the 'big boys' putting pressure on the smaller ones,' he said.

'Like Papa tried with you?'

'Probably. Everyone should have the right to choose.'

'Even Henri?'

Xavier frowned at the mention of their elder brother.

'It's a bit different with him. If he wants there to be any of the business left for him to inherit, he had better stop his gambling with the profits and start to plough some money back in. Papa is desperate over it all.'

Jocelyn laid her hand gently on his arm. 'He wants you back in the business. Can't you come back, just to oblige him?'

Xavier shook his head. 'I've never made any pretence of wanting to join the family business. It's not in my line, and I'd find it impossible to work with Henri. No, Papa will have to have it out with Henri and draw up some clear lines of responsibility. He knows he's living beyond his means, and thinks he knows how he's managing it.'

He looked cynically at his sister, his lips grimacing slightly. 'I called to see Henri on my way here. He was very much on edge. Papa could be right about him. What do you think?'

Jocelyn laughed shortly. 'I'm the last

one Henri would take into his confidence. Brother or not, he knows I've no sympathies with him. Anyway, enough of Henri and his machinations, let's get this place tidy and then you can take me to this windmill and I can give you my opinion of it, and your new 'model',' she added mischievously.

Xavier tried to laugh dismissively, but winced with the effort. He shook his head at her former suggestion. He wanted to get on with the inspection of the windmill.

In spite of the pain of each movement as he got out of the car by the windmill, Xavier had temporarily forgotten how awful he looked. Lys's gasp as she saw him reminded him.

'Xavier! What's happened?'

'I ran into three thugs who didn't like the look of me,' he replied lightly, not wanting to delay Jocelyn's inspection of the windmill.

Lys's eyes were drawn to the attractive young woman who had driven Xavier here. She was beautiful. What an extraordinary friendship they must have. Xavier looking like a free spirit of nature and this immaculately dressed women who might have stepped straight out of a fashion magazine!

'Lys, meet Jocelyn, my, er, friend from back home.'

Lys noticed that he seemed to throw Jocelyn a warning glance about something. Did they have a relationship going that they wished to keep private? The disparity of their appearance made it seem unlikely, but who could tell? Opposites often attracted each other.

She reached out her hand as Xavier continued, 'Jocelyn, this is Lys, the miller's granddaughter. Shall we say hello to your grandfather first, Lys?'

'Yes. He's keeping awake specially. Come this way, mademoiselle.'

'Oh, call me Jocelyn, Lys. A friend of Xavier's is a friend of mine!'

Hmm, so there was something between them! Lys felt another spark of jealousy but tried to quell it.

She saw Xavier wince as he stepped

forward and she reached out to touch his arm.

'You're really hurting! Come and sit down inside. Never mind about the windmill today. There's no hurry.'

Xavier made his twisted grin. He was touched by the concern he could read in her face. Her fingers felt cool on his arm and he wondered if she would be able to soothe away the aches in his body. Unfortunately, it wasn't the right opportunity to find out.

'Sitting, standing, lying down, it makes no difference. I'll take some more painkillers in ten minutes or so. I'm all right.'

Fortunately, the poor light in Etienne's bedroom hid his injuries from the older man's sight and, after a few words of introduction and Etienne's appreciation for Jocelyn's time, they left Etienne to go to sleep and went over to the windmill.

Lys found it interesting to hear the professional jargon as Xavier and Jocelyn discussed the condition of the windmill and the likelihood of trickery by Leon Boudot. Xavier let Jocelyn arrive at her own conclusions and they were both relieved when her judgment agreed with Xavier's.

'I've got my laptop in my car and I'll make out a report this evening,' she promised. 'You can take it to the Hotel de Ville as soon as it opens on Tuesday morning. I'll write a separate report on the likelihood of the cause of the stairs falling and describe the evidence. Don't let Boudot handle it. If he's guilty, which I'm sure he is, he'll know how damning it is and I'm sure he'll back down. There'll be no claims for injuries on your property. In fact, I advise you to make a counter claim for damages from him. He might fight it but the damage needs to be repaired and will add extra costs.'

Lys was grateful for their help and advice. She invited them both to stay for a light meal but Jocelyn insisted that she take Xavier back with her and get him to bed.

Xavier made no move to desist and it tore at Lys's heart to see him painfully manoeuvre himself into Jocelyn's car. She reluctantly waved them off and returned to the windmill to bring Grandpère up to date with their assessment, wishing it were she who was to take care of Xavier instead of Jocelyn. The more she saw of him, the more she liked him but she realised her newly found attraction to him was unlikely to lead anywhere.

She pulled a wry face. From their relaxed way with each other, Xavier and Jocelyn knew each other well, friends from home, Xavier had said, and still in touch with each other. It must mean they were more than just friends.

It was late when she retired to her room and went to bed. She spent time going over her plans for the windmill, and time wistfully dreaming of romance with Xavier.

She was just drifting off to sleep when a horrid thought struck her. What if Xavier had been attacked because of his involvement with the mill? Had Leon Boudot discovered Xavier's intention to help them? If so, it was all her fault.

6

Since Grandpère hadn't noticed Xavier's injuries, Lys didn't confide her worries to him. She collected fresh croissants and rolls from Madame Giraud and told her she was going into Le Château to the Sunday market and would be getting some mussels and prawns for tea and would she like to come and join them?

Madame Giraud thanked her for the invitation but said she always used the opportunity of closing at lunchtime on Sundays to visit her friends. Today she was going to visit one at La Continiere, a fishing port a few kilometres north of Vertbois.

Lys decided to go in her car, though once out on the road she doubted the wisdom of her choice, as the traffic was unusually heavy. Of course. It was the holiday weekend. Hundreds of day-trippers were flowing on to the island.

She parked where the road from Ors met the road to the port but went to the market first to buy the moules and crevettes, which she stored in a coolbox in the boot of her car and then drove down the road to Xavier's hut.

She was surprised to find him up and busy with a long-handled broom, though she could tell that every moment gave him pain.

'Let me do that,' she pleaded, reaching out for the broom.

'Lys! Salut!'

He looked pleased to see her, Lys noted with pleasure. 'If you hold the shovel for me,' he continued, 'it will be a great help! Bending is still a bit difficult.'

'Er, is Jocelyn still here?' Lys was curious to know, as she picked up the shovel. 'Did she stay overnight?'

'Not in here.' Xavier grinned, his smile less painful today. 'A bit too basic for Jocelyn.'

'Mmm, and for most women,' Lys agreed, glancing around at the lack of comfort. There wasn't much left apart from the debris on the floor. 'Is everything ruined?'

'More or less. I can salvage some of the wood and knock up a couple of easels but the paint is ruined and all my paper. I'll have to get more on Tuesday.'

'Do you know why they did it, Xavier?'

He shook his head. 'I haven't a clue! I'm wondering if they mistook me for someone else.'

'Do you think it might be because of me?' Lys asked hesitantly.

'Because of you?' he echoed in amazement. 'Why on earth should that be?'

She spread her hands. 'Maybe Boudot knows you're helping us? Maybe it was to frighten you off?'

She looked so downcast that Xavier put his hands on her shoulders and then gently tilted her chin up towards him. Her face, as she looked up at him was so anxious that he smiled tenderly and shook his head. He would have loved to kiss her, but he feared his lips were still too painful and he wanted to enjoy it to the full when the proper occasion arose.

'Whatever their motive, it was nothing to do with you or your grandfather's windmill,' he assured her. 'They kept saying, 'What have you done with it?' but I've no idea what they were talking about. That's why I think it might have been a case of mistaken identity.'

She felt vastly relieved. 'I hardly slept all night.'

'Don't tell me that my ugly face gave you nightmares.' He grinned.

'Sort of!' she grinned back, vastly relieved to hear Xavier's assessment of the situation. 'That's why I've dashed round here.'

'And I thought it was to help me sweep out my hut.'

The pseudo-downcast expression on his face made her heart leap and beat uncontrollably.

'That, too!' She laughed, wanting him to know she cared, even if his thoughts for her were purely platonic.

They worked in harmony until everything worth salvaging had been neatly stacked to one side and everything else swept into a plastic bin-bag. Lys then looked questioningly at Xavier.

'What are you going to do with yourself for the rest of the day? Did you say Jocelyn was still in town?'

'I didn't say, but, no, she's not. I persuaded her to go back to her holiday on Ile de Ré, I didn't want her fussing over me like a mother hen.'

Lys doubted that Jocelyn's fussing would have been motherly!

'I wondered if you felt up to a drive around part of the island. It would give you a general idea of the place and you can return at your leisure on your bicycle when you don't hurt quite so much.'

★　★　★

As they drove along, she pointed out the start of a cycle path that veered away from the road just before Le Petit Village.

Just farther on, another path on the left went to the town's small port and then a cycle track along the sea edge to the wide boulevard that led to the Yachting Club.

She drove slowly along the boulevard and through the pretty town of St. Trojan that rivalled any Mediterranean village in Lys's opinion, drinking in the almost-forgotten sights.

She stopped at a small café and bought some sandwiches.

'Let's eat them on the beach. I've been here three days and haven't seen the Atlantic waves yet. We'll go down to Le Grand Plage. There's an old wreck there that was washed ashore years ago. It might make an interesting sketch.'

The roar of the Atlantic, rushing ashore crested with frothing foam, greeted them as they topped the rise of the sand-dunes. A few surfers were riding the waves and other holiday-makers were splashing about in the shallower water.

'Do you surf?' she asked Xavier, thinking he probably did.

'Yes, but not right now. The very thought of flinging myself on to a board makes me wince.'

'Sorry! We could swim though, couldn't we? I've got my bikini on under my shorts. What about you. The salty water will be good for your bruises.'

They picked their way over the hot sand, through the family groups and children building sandcastles, until they reached a more secluded area.

'Swim first, and sandwiches after!' Lys suggested, dropping the beach mats on to the sand. 'Come on! I'll race you!'

She knew Xavier still found move-ment painful but she guessed he would find it worse if she were solicitously waiting on him. As it was, he had pulled off his shirt and shorts before she had and was legging it down towards the sea.

With a cry of, 'Wait for me!' she ran after him and caught up with him in the shallow water. She gasped at the sight of his back, chest and legs and was glad that she was still behind him so that he couldn't see the concern on her face. The bruises glared angrily through his tan, making her wonder how he managed to stifle the pain he must be in.

To ease her embarrassment, she threw a handful of water at him.

Xavier turned to return the splash but Lys dived into the next wave, gasping at the sudden chill to her body. They frolicked in the waves for ten minutes or so, ending when they surfaced near together.

'Had enough?' Xavier teased, taking hold of both of Lys's hands.

The humour in his voice was suddenly belied by the expression in his eyes and Lys wasn't surprised when he drew her towards him until their bodies were touching. He released her hands and cupped each side of her face.

'You're very beautiful,' he whispered. 'Maybe I shouldn't, but I want to kiss you.'

Lys felt the same, and he had said that he and Jocelyn were old friends. Maybe that's all they were to each other? She certainly had no-one special to think about. She lifted her face and they gently kissed. Electric tingles ran through Lys's body and she yearned for a deeper kiss.

Instead, Xavier lessened the pressure, but he ran his lips along her jaw line and down her neck, making her shiver with delight. As they drew apart, Xavier smiled.

'That was exquisite pain!' he joked.

She wasn't sure if he was referring to his relationship with Jocelyn or the tenderness of his body, and didn't want to know if it were the former.

'That's OK,' she said lightly, just in case he was thinking of Jocelyn.

They casually linked fingers as they

splashed back through the warm shallow water and headed back up the beach to where they had left their few belongings. Lys felt exhilarated by the swim and by the physical contact with Xavier.

She dropped on to one of the beach mats and rubbed at her hair with her towel, glad she had thought to put it in the car.

'You were right about the sea being good for my bruises. I feel better already.'

Lys heart leaped with pleasure. 'We must do it again tomorrow, then. That is . . .'

Her voice trailed away as Xavier's eyes broke contact and he lowered himself carefully on to the other mat. Lys handed him a sandwich, wishing she hadn't assumed too much.

'I got you tuna. I thought it would be easier for you to eat. Is that all right?' she babbled, hoping to distract him.

'Fine! Mmm! It's good.'

He leaned on one elbow and turned

towards her. 'Lys?'

She knew she had to face it. 'Mmm?'

'Don't get serious about me. I like you and you're fun to be with, but I'm here to work. I've set myself a heavy schedule and I can't afford to mess it up. D'you know what I'm saying?'

She felt she knew. He didn't mind a bit of fun but no strings attached. Well, so what? Maybe that was all she wanted? She certainly wasn't looking for anything long-term, not with her restoration project on the go.

'That suits me,' she said lightly. 'I'll be pretty busy myself. Is that why you sent Jocelyn away?'

'Jocelyn? Yeh, you've got it. Great girl, isn't she?'

There was something in his tone she wasn't quite sure of but, when she looked straight into his eyes, they were tender, and it made her realise that he must feel a great deal for Jocelyn.

'Yes,' she agreed, reluctantly acknowledging the truth of it. Jocelyn was nice, though Lys wished she weren't. But,

Jocelyn wasn't here, and she, Lys, was. And she felt a strong attraction to him, in spite of Jocelyn.

She decided to be frank. 'I like you. I didn't at first! I was annoyed at the way you said you thought I didn't have enough about me to be independent from my rich step-father. Maybe I've never had a purpose before. I have now. And I'm going to make it work.'

Eventually they ate their sandwiches, kissed some more and then agreed to continue the tour of the area. They were physically relaxed together and walked back to the car with their arms around each other's waist. Lys felt she had known him all her life, or was it that her life had begun when she first met him?

As she drove the car up the coast through Le Grand Village, past Vertbois, to La Perroche and then the port of La Cotiniere, she was aware that he was seated partly sideways, his eyes smilingly resting on her face, as if he were memorising every detail.

He was. Her features fascinated him.

Her skin was smooth and soft to the touch, and he now touched her with his eyes. Her hair was swept off her face by the breeze through the windows and her eyes were full of love.

The afternoon was drawing on. Neither wanted to part but Lys knew her grandfather would be expecting her back home again.

'Would you like to come for something to eat?' she asked suddenly. 'I bought some prawns and mussels from the market this morning. There are plenty for three. And we'll have some of Madame Giraud's fresh bread and salad.'

Xavier's heart eased with pleasure. 'That's an offer I can't refuse!'

Grandpère decided he wanted to join them in the main living-room and, after some consideration, Lys and Xavier helped him through.

They discussed various options of how to go about renovating the windmill and Grandpère said he knew the very man to renew any woodwork.

'He re-laid the upper floor just before Marlene died,' he said, with a faraway look in his eyes. 'I have since thought I had wasted my money, but not now,' he added with resolution. 'I shouldn't have given up so easily, but it's time to move on. I'll see those sails turning again before I die.'

Lys took Xavier back to Le Château and arranged to pick him up at ten o'clock in the morning to continue the tour of the island.

It was another enjoyable day and it passed all too quickly. When Lys and Xavier parted, they made only general plans as to when they would next see each other.

'Let me know how you get on at the municipal office tomorrow,' Xavier said.

'I will, and I hope you have no difficulty setting up your studio again.'

Lys woke early on Tuesday morning. She ate a hasty breakfast and saw that Grandpère had his tray to hand. Then she drove to St. Pierre, the municipal centre of the island and managed to get the first appointment in the Clerk of Works' office.

Their application for a grant was received with some surprise. 'But there is already an application for demolishing the windmill and building a supermarket on the site,' the man told her. 'You are sure you have the correct information, mademoiselle?'

'Of course I have. My grandpère owns the mill. He still lives in it. It's been in the family for over a hundred years!'

'And he has not sold to Monsieur Fayau?'

'No! There has been some pressure on him to make him do so, but we have had our own independent survey done and the windmill is in good condition. We want to apply for a grant to renovate it and make it into a working museum. I've made enquiries and there isn't a working windmill on the island that is open to the public.'

The clerk was reading Jocelyn's report as Lys talked and comparing it to another report already in his file.

'There seems to be some discrepancies here, mademoiselle. Leon Boudot does not seem to share your optimistic view of the situation. Wait here whilst I make some enquiries.'

Lys waited anxiously. She knew their application was sound, but would Boudot's exaggerations of the defects take precedence over Jocelyn's since he was one of the authority's surveyors?

When the clerk returned, he was frowning. 'You say that Monsieur Dupont still lives in the windmill, and has no intention of selling it, mademoiselle?'

'That's correct.'

'Well, there seems to be some confusion here. The area surveyor seems to have overstepped his brief. This is quite irregular.'

'Will our application for a grant be considered, do you think?'

The clerk read the survey again, pursing his lips. 'I don't see why not. There are forms to fill in, of course, and it could take some months, unless, of course, it goes on to the priority list because of its potential, and to offset its mishandling,' he added as he noticed the disappointment in Lys's face.

'I will do what I can for you, mademoiselle, and will send another surveyor around as soon as possible.'

'Will it be all right for us to start work on things that we can do ourselves?' Lys thought to ask.

'By all means. If I can remember the place correctly, it was always a well-kept, attractive concern. That was in Madame Dupont's time, of course, before Etienne let it go.'

'Grandpère is very keen to see it restored now,' Lys was pleased to tell him. She bestowed a beaming smile on him. 'With your help, it shouldn't be too long.'

Lys drove back to the windmill. The sight of Leon Boudot's car sobered her excitement, but she was determined not to let the man know it.

She could hear his raised voice as she

opened the door. 'This is your last chance to sell at a good price, you old fool! Fayau won't be repeating his offer, I can tell you! He has his eye on other sites as well as this one!'

'Then tell him to make his offer on one of those!' Etienne replied with spirit.

'You're forgetting my claim for recompense for personal injury caused by neglect of your property!' Boudot snapped. 'The fine will ruin you!'

'I doubt that very much!' Lys said quietly behind him.

He whirled round to face her, sneering at her words. 'What do you know about such matters? I already have a doctor's certificate to prove my injuries.'

'Then you either exaggerated your injuries, or misled him as to the cause.'

'You were there, mademoiselle. You saw the stairway collapse. It was unsafe, and demolition is the only answer.'

'Not according to the surveyor's report I have just lodged at the municipal building in St. Pierre, monsieur! Our independent surveyor gave the windmill an excellent report.'

'Impossible! It has been the holiday weekend. No-one works over the holidays.'

'It was done by a friend of a friend.'

'I shall challenge it! It has been done in your favour.'

'Don't worry. The clerk at St. Pierre is going to send an independent surveyor to check. And, curiously, our surveyor found evidence of crucial wood-screws having been removed shortly before the collapse of the steps.'

She watched his face and was pleased to see a shadow of apprehension darken his eyes.

'Nonsense!' he sneered. 'You're lying!'

'No, Monsieur Boudot, I'm not lying, and you know it!'

Her legs were shaking but her voice was firm.

'You'll regret this, mademoiselle!' Boudot threatened.

'I doubt it, Monsieur Boudot. Now, I

must bid you good day! My grandpère and I have plans to make.'

Boudot snapped his lips together and, after a momentary hesitation, he swung on his heels and stalked back to his car. Lys watched in satisfaction as he drove away.

She relayed to her grandpère all that the municipal clerk had said to her and was pleased to see the light of excitement glow in his eyes.

'And we can start some of the work straightaway, Grandpère. We've only to leave the bits that we need the grant for, like rebuilding the sails and renewing the stairways. Oh, and building public toilets and a car park, apparently, that is required by law, but we can get someone to re-point the stonework, redo the rendering and do all the paintwork, only we're to keep the bills to show how much money we are putting into the venture.

'So, as soon as we've had a cup of coffee, you can make a list of people to contact to give us some quotes, and I'm going to start pulling up some weeds. I'll just get some gloves I keep under the passenger seat of my car.'

She grimaced. 'My step-father insisted I learn how to change a tyre.'

She wasn't really grumbling. Oscar had been very generous with her, with little appreciation shown in return, she had to admit.

She went out to her car, opened the rear door and felt under the seat for the protective gloves she knew was there. As her fingers identified the texture of them, she also felt the unfamiliar texture of a tightly-wrapped package, and she drew it out.

It was something enclosed in a clear plastic bag that had been folded over many times and secured with elastic bands. She had never seen it before and was puzzled as to how it had become lodged under the passenger seat of her car.

Maybe its contents would throw light on the matter?

She removed the elastic bands and

unrolled the bag. A slim black leather box was inside. The sort you would expect to find a necklace in. Curious to see if she were right, she undid the clasp and opened the box.

Her eyes widened in surprise.

She was no expert at identifying precious jewellery, but she had no doubt in her mind whatsoever that what she held in her hands was the most exquisitely beautiful necklace she had ever seen.

7

Lys felt bewildered. What was it doing in her car? It hadn't been there when she had packed her belongings in Paris. She'd had the garage do a full valet service. They wouldn't have missed this.

The only other person who had been in her car since then was Xavier. But what would he be doing with such an expensive item of jewellery? And why hadn't he asked her for it? Surely, if it were his, he would have wondered where it was by now? Unless the attack on him had pushed it out of his mind?

A sudden thought struck her mind. What if this were what the thieves were after? What was it he had said they kept shouting at him? 'What have you done with it?' Or, 'Where is it?' Did Xavier think they had eventually found it? Was that why he hadn't mentioned it? He knew it was missing but thought the thieves had taken it?

He'd be relieved to have it back again, then, wouldn't he? Or, would he?

She looked at it spread across her hand. The rainbow of colour from its many facets took her breath away. It must be worth a fortune! What would a penniless artist be doing with a piece of jewellery like this?

A frown darkened her face. Had he come by it dishonestly?

She instinctively shied away from the idea, but how much did she know of him? Not very much, if the truth were known. He had shared far less of himself than she had shared with him. She knew nothing about his past, his family, his friends, apart from Jocelyn, and that was an incongruous friendship. One so obviously well-to-do, wearing designer clothes, and one living on the edge of poverty, compelled to paint for his living.

Did the necklace belong to Jocelyn? But Jocelyn hadn't been in her car. She couldn't have dropped it.

113

Maybe Xavier had it in his possession to give to Jocelyn? Maybe it needed some attention that Xavier could provide through his contacts?

No, there was more to it than that? He would have missed it. It would surely have occurred to him to suspect it was in Lys's car. Unless, for some reason, he didn't want to mention it, didn't want Lys to know anything about it.

She sighed in exasperation. What was she to do? If she returned it openly, he might feel compelled to give a false reason for it being in his possession, and she didn't want him to lie to her. She couldn't bear to think of there being an air of restraint between them.

So, should she contrive to somehow return it to his hut without him knowing who had put it there? But, if he said noting about it to her, she would forever wonder why not.

She could take it to the police and let them ask the questions. But, they'd want to know who had been in her car, and that would take their enquiries straight to Xavier. She would feel she had betrayed him.

She was startled to suddenly realise that all her thoughts were presuming the necklace to have come into Xavier's hands dishonestly, and that her preoccupation with what to do about it was her desire to shield him from the consequences.

She could challenge him, however awkward it made things between them. But something made her hold back. Something about the necklace niggled at the back of her mind. It was of a heavy lace-work pattern. She had a sudden flashback memory of seeing it displayed against a black velvet background. But, where? Why?

Who might know? She thought of one of her university friends, Robert Devreux. He might know. He had studied design in jewellery. He might recognise a drawing of the necklace.

Surprisingly, she managed to push her concern of the diamond necklace to the back of her mind and, with her Grandpère sitting in a chair in the doorway of the cottage watching her work, she spent two busy hours pulling out weeds, tying some tall hollyhocks to some small pegs in the wall and trimming back some shrubs that had made a take-over bid.

It was back-breaking work and she was glad when Etienne suggested she stop and make them both a cool drink.

Grandpère had compiled a list of likely small businesses that would be capable of doing the smaller jobs for them. He had written down at least two possibilities for each job.

'Let them know there's competition for them,' he told Lys. 'Make them a bit keener to keep the price down.'

Not one to sit around when she was eager to see the renovation work begin, as soon as she knew businesses would be reopened after the lunchtime break, Lys set off to speak to the proprietors in person. It was a tiring afternoon but at the end of it she had two businesses interested in each of the sections of work required.

'Availability will count as much as price,' she warned them, and was pleased to hear the good opinion of her grandfather from the majority of them.

Exultant with the success of her mission she returned to share the results with her grandfather.

Etienne looked at the amended list, while Lys cooked a quick omelette for both of them, alternately pursing his lips and nodding his head.

'Not bad, not bad,' he allowed. 'You've done a good job, Lysette.'

Lys was pleased with his praise but found herself dwelling more on her concern over the diamond necklace as they ate their meal.

'You're quiet, Lysette,' Grandpère commented. 'Go and see what the artistic friend of your is up to.'

'Yes, I might do that,' Lys responded. She would confront Xavier with the necklace and give him a chance to explain what it was doing in her car.

Relieved to have made that decision, she cleared away the remnants of their meal and went to change into shorts and vest top.

She took the diamond necklace out of the bottom of her wardrobe and weighed the packet thoughtfully in her hand. She wouldn't take it with her. She didn't want to risk losing it or having it stolen. She pushed it into one of her shoes and put it back into the wardrobe. It should be safe there.

It was early evening as she drove into Le Château and holidaymakers were thronging the streets, looking for evening entertainment.

Lys turned towards the port and parked on the spare piece of land near the fishing huts. She could see Xavier sitting in the doorway of his studio-hut, swiftly sketching the portrait of a young lady. She paused on the fringe of the group around him, knowing that he was so intent on his work that she would remain unnoticed.

She enjoyed watching him, admiring

the swift, deft movements of his hands as he sketched and shaded, accurately recording the penetrating discernment of his eyes.

The sitter's friends were watching in admiration, whether at Xavier's skill of his personal attributes, she was unable to decide. His bruises gave him a roguish air.

Xavier lifted his sketchpad, lightly blew upon it and then reached under his stool for an aerosol can, the contents of which he sprayed across his drawing, fixing the soft pastel medium. He smiled at his model and handed it towards her. Lys could see her pleasure and the delight with which she showed the portrait to her friends.

Xavier must have sensed her presence and he turned round, smiling a welcome.

The warmth of his smile stirred Lys's heart, temporarily relegating to the recesses of her mind the reservations she had been nurturing. She smiled back, aware that the next would-be model had taken her place upon the sitter's stool.

'I'll look around the other studios,' she said lightly. 'See you later.'

Her thoughts kept returning to the diamond necklace as she sauntered in seeming carefree mood around the cluster of simple studios.

When at length she returned to Xavier's studio, she found he was still busy employed sketching portraits. He shrugged his shoulders slightly, his glance encompassing his waiting clients.

Lys smiled with understanding. Knowing how important his work was, she didn't want to distract him or make him think she was waiting impatiently.

'I'll wander down to the port for a while,' she mouthed, nodding her head in the right direction. 'I like it down there.'

She strolled past the restaurants, appreciating the breeze that blew against her face and slowly sauntered to the far end of the jetty. Her mind wandered to their plans for the windmill and she leisurely explored various possibilities, some including Xavier's participation in some measure. A slight sound behind her broke into her reverie and she turned to find the subject of her thoughts putting the finishing touches to his sketchpad.

'I couldn't resist,' he smiled. 'I hope you don't mind. I've been wanting to draw you since we met.'

He held out the pad and she took it from his hand. The sketch was her profile, her expression serious yet musingly thoughtful. A tiny smile played at the corner of her mouth and she felt her cheeks redden as she wondered which of her thoughts had provoked it, and did Xavier guess?

She thought of her decision to try to clarify the ownership of the necklace and scrambled to her feet in some confusion.

'Very nice,' she complimented him a little more brusquely than she had intended.

'Er, have you finished for the evening?' she asked diffidently.

'Yes, I have done well today.'

He patted his pocket. 'Enough to treat us to some supper. Where do you recommend?'

'Oh!' She didn't want him to spend his well-earned money on her. 'Shouldn't you save it, buy some new materials with it?'

Xavier's eyebrows rose slightly as he smiled in return. 'I have put most of it on one side. This . . . ' patting his pocket again, 'this is to spend, to enjoy. I want to spend some money on you. What is the point of money if you can't enjoy it?'

Lys wondered how easily money ran through his fingers. Did he supplement his income by other illicit means? Ashamed of her thoughts, she spoke quickly. 'As long as you're sure.' She gave a nervous laugh. 'It's none of my business, really, how you spend your money. I'll, er, go halves with you.'

Unaware of her inner turmoil, Xavier

took hold of her hand. 'Not tonight! Tonight I will pay! Tomorrow? Who knows? Now, where shall we go?'

'One of the fish restaurants? I've eaten with Grandpère, so I'm not very hungry. We could share a plate of sea food, if you like.'

They chose the restaurant called *L'Etoile de La Mer*, 'The Star of the Sea', and Xavier ordered the food and a bottle of wine. He had chosen an excellent bottle and Lys sipped it appreciatively.

Not wanting to put a dampener of the evening, Lys decided to wait until later before she quizzed him and her initial nervousness was soon dispelled by Xavier's ease of small talk, helped, no doubt, by the wine.

The waiter carried aloft a large platter of sea food to their table and placed it with a flourish on their table.

'Bon appetite!' he wished them, as he withdrew.

'Mmm, oysters. I love them,' Xavier murmured as she glanced over the platter. He indicated to Lys that she take one. 'Do you like them?' he asked as he loosened the muscle that held the delicacy in its shell.

'I've never had one,' Lys admitted, eyeing them doubtfully. 'When I came here as a child I never thought they looked very appetising.'

Xavier laughed. 'This is what you do.'

He held out the shell to his lips between his thumb and second finger, tilted back his head and let the creamy-coloured creature slide down his throat.

'Your turn, now.' Xavier encouraged her.

Lys grinned at him. 'This had better be good.'

She copied his action, aware the Xavier was closely watching her, and was surprised how good it felt. She reached out for another.

'They could become addictive. I always thought they were expensive.'

'In Paris, and around the world, they are. But this area specialises in them and provides over a third of the world trade. Here they are part of the staple diet, like the rest of this platter.'

'We used to collect as many of these as we could,' Lys reminisced, looking at the clams and palourds, the cockles and mussels, periwinkles and others she had forgotten the names. 'Then we would make a bed of large stones, put the shellfish on the stones and pile dry grass on top. Then we'd set fire to the grass and wait for the shells to open, then we would eat them. Maman was more fun in those days, when Papa was always around.' Her expression saddened. 'I don't know who changed first, whether it was Maman or Papa. Whoever it was, they drifted apart and Papa began to stay away longer each time he left. I sometimes felt Maman drove him away, but I don't know.'

Xavier reached out and laid his hand over hers. 'People change, ma cherie. It is not always someone's fault. It just happens. You will change. I will change. The island will change.'

Lys managed to smile at that. 'It hasn't changed much in the past fifty years.'

'But it is changing now. That's why your idea of a museum of the history of the windmills will catch people's interest. Tell me how you're getting on. Has Boudot been around to see you?'

'He has indeed.'

Lys proceeded to tell him all that had happened since she had seen him last and time slipped away as they companionably ate and talked. After the bill had been paid and they emerged into the cool night air, she knew that she could put off asking about his knowledge of the necklace no longer.

Xavier slid his arm around her waist and drew her close, gently kissing her. Lys responded, savouring the kiss, wishing she didn't have to risk spoiling their growing friendship. It felt so right with him. It ended when they both needed to breathe.

'Have you cleared all the debris away now?' Lys asked, tentatively steering the

126

conversation towards the mugging. 'Have you missed anything else that might have been stolen?'

'Yes, to the first, and no to the second,' Xavier answered without pause.

Was it too quickly, she wondered?

'Nothing of value?' she pressed.

'My paintings were of value.'

'Yes, of course. I meant anything else?'

'Such as?'

Lys was suddenly wary. She wondered if she detected an edge to his voice. Did he suspect where her questions were leading?

'Oh, I don't know, your watch? A camera? Anything personal?' A diamond necklace, she added silently. 'Whatever they were after.'

Xavier looked puzzled. 'I told you, I don't know what they were after. Maybe they didn't know either?' He shrugged. 'They took three of the best paintings I've ever done. But I don't think that's what they were after.'

Lys sensed the sincerity in his voice, but the necklace was real. She still couldn't decide for sure whether he knew about it or not, she needed to know more about it before she revealed her knowledge of it.

8

The next few days passed slowly for Lys. She sent her drawing of the diamond necklace to Robert Devereux, asking him to let her know what he thought of it, at the earliest opportunity.

She then turned her attention to the diamond necklace itself. Reluctant to have such an expensive item of jewellery lying around, she gave serious thought as to where she could keep it safely. A slow grin spread itself across her face as an idea came to her. Ideal!

A quick visit to Le Château got her all the materials that she needed, and, before the day was out, the necklace was safely concealed. No-one would find it without her help.

She kept herself busy tidying the rest of the land around the windmill. The hollyhocks and roses only needed room to grow and they would blossom. As would their plans for developing the living museum, she was sure.

Buoyed by this anticipation, she should have been happy and contented, but her heart felt heavy and she knew it was because of her concerns about Xavier's involvement in what might turn out to be an illegal operation. She didn't make any move to contact him, preferring to distance herself from him until she knew more about the necklace. Her enquiries seemed like a betrayal of him, and that didn't rest lightly on her shoulders.

Memories of his kisses made her long to see him again and she had to force herself to be strong to stay true to her resolve to stay away.

As each day went by without any of the businesses sending their representatives along to do the job, her excitement at getting the promises of the estimates began to fade.

'Why does no-one come?' she

demanded for the twentieth time. 'They seemed eager to have our business,' she said dismally.

On Wednesday, a phone call from Robert temporarily put their renovation plans on the backburner. She slipped outside to take the call in private.

Their greetings over, Lys got straight to the point. 'Was my drawing good enough, Robert? Do you recognise the setting?'

Robert laughed at her eagerness. 'Whoa! Whoa! Slow down a bit, Lys. Yes, I recognise it. It looks to me like the Monsigny Collar. It has been in the Monsigny family for a couple of centuries and ought to be at home in the Monsigny Château. There have been no reports of it having been stolen. Are you sure it's genuine? It could be a fake.'

Lys pulled her face. 'It looks real, but, then, a good fake would. Wouldn't it? I hadn't thought of that. Is it likely that there's a fake around?'

'Could be. A lot of valuable pieces

are copied. Their owners keep the genuine items safely in the vaults and wear the fakes.'

She suddenly felt that she had been reading too much into the incident. A fake necklace would hardly warrant much attention. Still, that would take Xavier out of suspicion of any crime, wouldn't it? Her spirit brightened.

Her recovered spirit didn't last long. Robert picked up on her disappointment and added, 'Of course, that doesn't explain why this guy of yours should have it in his possession. Whether he knew it's a fake or not, it's a bit suspicious that he has it at all! What's the connection?'

Lys shrugged. 'I don't know.'

Her mind ran swiftly over possibilities, none of them satisfactory. A fake was either a decoy or a fraud! Where did Xavier fit into either scene?

Lys's inner misgivings over the matter were pushed into the background by yet another day passing by with no-one coming to look at their requirements for the renovation of the windmill.

'I'm going to see what's holding them up, Grandpère,' she announced over lunch on Friday. 'If they didn't want the jobs, why didn't they say so?'

The first two proprietors she visited made uncomfortable apologies about unforeseen urgent work needed to be done elsewhere. The third proprietor, Pierre Auden, listened carefully to her now well-rehearsed questions and sighed heavily as he placed his hands on the table between them.

'I am sorry, Mademoiselle Dupont, but I have my business to think of. If I do work that is unlikely to be paid for . . . ' He shrugged his shoulders expressively. ' . . . I would soon be in trouble and be faced with closing down. I wish you and Etienne well, but I have to be realistic.'

Lys felt the colour drain out of her face, and then rush back in again. 'What do you mean?' she demanded. 'Grandpère would never be in debt to anyone, let alone to local businesses. He knows all about sailing close to the wind. His milling business folded through lack of trade, but he has no unpaid debts. We have gone through everything and, with the grant from the municipal authorities, everything will be paid for as it is done.'

The edges of Pierre's mouth pulled downwards as he shook his head.

'That's not what the local grapevine is saying. The word is out that there'll be no grant, and no funds to fall back on. I'm sorry, Mademoiselle.'

The shock Lys felt at his words showed clearly on her face. She gripped the edge of the table to steady herself.

'Who has told you this?'

Pierre shrugged slightly. 'As I said, the local grapevine. A number of people called me, Guerlain, Brieuc, Hillotte. All said the same thing.'

'But it's not true!' Lys protested. 'I have spoken with the clerk of works at St. Pierre. He was very encouraging and promised a swift passage through the necessary channels. I beg you to reconsider.'

'Nothing would please me more, Mademoiselle. Bring me written word from Etienne's bank and I will be delighted to submit an estimate.'

Lys retracted her steps to the two businesses she had already visited and, in response to her direct question, was the given the same answer. Someone had spread malicious rumours. Determined to discover the source, she visited the other businesses. Finally, Hillotte was willing to give a direct source.

'It was a young lady from the municipal bureau,' he admitted. 'She said she had heard you were touting around for estimates but that you had no chance of being granted necessary funds.'

Lys frowned. 'Is it usual practice for a municipal employee to do that?'

The same Gallic shrug proceeded Monsieur Hillotte's response. 'Not really. I took it as a piece of genuine advice and counted it a fortunate escape.'

'And passed it around the district?'

Hillotte had the grace to look ashamed. 'We stick together. No-one wants to see friend's businesses fail, even if they are competitors.'

'Very admirable.' Lys snorted. 'You would do better to check the facts first. Do you realise my grandfather could sue you for slander?'

Hillotte looked regretful. 'I repeat my apology, mademoiselle. The source seemed genuine. It was the municipal office.'

Lys shook her head. 'It couldn't be! There is no foundation for the rumour.'

Lys glanced at her watch, pleased to see that she had time to get to St. Pierre before closing time. She cycled home, left her bicycle and transferred to her car. This had to be sorted.

Brushing aside all efforts from the receptionist to insist on her making an appointment, Lys eventually entered the chief clerk's office and laid her complaint before him.

At the end of her tale, he instantly begged leave of her and disappeared into the inner office. It was five minutes before he returned.

'My enquiries have been unsuccessful in discovering any such phone call from these premises, mademoiselle. The only other people with access to this request for a grant are my secretary, whose word I trust beyond all reproach, and Boudot, who is not in today. I find it hard to believe that he would jeopardise his career in this way. However, I will pursue the matter with him and let you know the results.'

He peered at her over his spectacles. 'In the meantime, let me tell you that your application is being seen to right now and I am sure you will be receiving good news some time next week. I believe your project will indeed bring much interest to the area and give us the boost we need in the tourist trade. Now, how about an official note from me to take round to these building businesses you have mentioned?'

He smiled kindly at her. 'I assure you, mademoiselle, I will do all I can get to the root of this matter. Leave it with me.'

Lys knew at whose door she would lay the first enquiries. Leon Boudot had the motive of revenge and was ruthless enough to do it. But, without proof, she wasn't prepared to accuse him. He would issue writs of slander if her accusations were unfounded, of that she was certain.

Satisfied that she had done all she could, Lys took her leave of him and once more revisited the appropriate businesses with the clerk's notice of approval, receiving assurances of swift quotations being prepared from all concerned.

Her grandfather greeted her arrival home with news that Xavier had called in to see him and had made his initial sketches of both him and the windmill.

'He's a likeable fellow,' Grandpère commented. 'I think he has missed you over the past few days. Not had an argument with him, have you?'

'No, nothing like that. I've been busy, that's all,' Lys assured him, feeling guilty at having to conceal her true reasons from him. At least she could now reveal what she had been doing all afternoon.

Needless to say, Etienne was appalled by her news, upset that someone had spread malicious lies about his solvency, and that his friends and neighbours of many years had been willing to believe his lies without checking first with him.

'Did they think I would cheat them?' he demanded, sinking into his chair.

Lys felt concerned about him. She didn't want this to cause another heart attack. She wished she hadn't told him what she had discovered.

'They were worried about their own businesses,' she pacified him. 'They obviously felt too embarrassed to check with you.'

Lys didn't know whether to be sorry

or glad that she had missed Xavier's visit. She longed to see him again but felt that her motives would be wrong if she were the one to seek him out, unless she were also prepared to ask him about his possession of the necklace.

They had been unsuccessful in their first attempt. Would they try again? And, if so, what would they do next? Was Xavier aware that he might be in danger? Perhaps she ought to warn him?

She had a disturbed sleep that night, dreaming of being chased through innumerable streets in a city she didn't know and awakened on Saturday morning determined to visit Xavier at Le Château.

Just after ten o'clock, two building contractors came in person to see what needed doing at the windmill, one to see to the work in the interior and the other to look at the outer rendering and paintwork. Both were effusive with their apologies for taking heed to the unfounded slur on Etienne's character and promised favourable estimations for the necessary work.

Another prospective worker came mid-afternoon, bearing apology from his employer, followed by yet another less than an hour later. Both eventually took their leave, promising early estimates. Things were looking promising and Etienne went to lie down, before preparing to visit Madame Giraud for his evening meal.

Lys had been invited but she declined with thanks. 'I might drive into Le Château,' she excused herself. 'We need some shopping and I might, er.'

'Visit your young man?' Etienne enquired with a smile.

'He's not my young man!' Lys denied, her face blushing.

'Of course not,' Grandpère agreed. 'Enjoy yourself, and don't worry about me. Madame Giraud will take good care of me.'

Lys drove to Le Château, did some necessary shopping and then drove round towards the port. As expected, Xavier was seated outside his studio, painting portraits again.

He smiled a welcome, making Lys's heart beat faster. His eyes seemed to linger hungrily upon her and she had to remind herself that he might not be the innocent artist he claimed to be. She smiled briefly and turned her gaze to the sketches exhibited around the inner walls of the wooden studio and on the doors. There was a variety of sketches . . . and one of their windmill.

Her heart filled with pleasure. It looked attractive, even in its dilapidated state. He hadn't doctored it to make it look grander than it was. It was there, warts and all. But beautiful to her eyes.

She was aware of someone's presence behind her and knew it was Xavier. She could feel his breath on her neck as he looked over her shoulder.

'Do you like it?' he asked, smiling at her.

'Oh, yes. You've captured it just right. Can I buy it?' she asked impulsively.

'For you, it is a gift,' Xavier said, unpinning the sketch and handing it to her.

'No, no! I must pay for it!' Lys insisted, embarrassed by his generosity.

'I have drawn more,' Xavier said lightly. 'The cost of paper and charcoal is minimal. Please accept it.'

'Thank you. I'll treasure it always,' she assured him.

'And here is your water well,' Xavier pointed out, 'and here . . . '

'Grandpère!'

'Indeed it was! He was sitting in the doorway of his cottage, his eyes full of his dream of the future. Hope, expectancy and love shone out of him.

'Oh, Xavier!'

She swallowed hard, fighting the lump in her throat and the threat of tears in her eyes.

'It is also for you . . . eventually,' Xavier told her. 'At the moment, it is my working sketch. See.'

He moved to a covered easel and lifted the cloth that hung upon it. The beginnings of a painted portrait smiled out at her. It bore excellent likeness to Etienne but she knew that more of his character would eventually be portrayed there. She nodded her pleasure.

'It's splendid!' she breathed softly, turning her eyes from the portrait of Xavier. He was standing very close and she could feel the warmth of his body through her thin summer dress. He touched her arm, sending electric tingles through her body.

'Are you staying until later?' Xavier asked. 'I've missed you this week.'

His dark brown eyes seemed like pools of melted chocolate and Lys felt her reservations about him fading away as she drowned in their depths. She flicked her eyelashes down momentarily, trying to recapture her sanity, but she knew it was too late for that. Xavier Piquet had stolen her heart and she didn't care how he had come into possession of the diamond necklace, legally or illegally.

'Yes,' she said softly, turning to face

him. Her hands had risen and were placed against his chest. She could feel his heartbeat. It seemed to match her own. 'Grandpère has been invited to tea at Madame Giraud's,' she added. 'He'll be all right.'

'Good!' Xavier whispered, as he lowered his head and placed his mouth gently over hers. His hands drew her closer still, moulding their bodies together.

She loved him.

No matter that he had said he wanted only a summer romance with no strings attached, she had fallen in love. Even though heartache might lie ahead, there was no turning back.

9

Lys made the instant decision to tell Xavier about the diamond necklace being in her car and that she had hidden it until she knew what to do with it, but was forestalled from mentioning it by the arrival of a potential client calling, 'Cooee!' from the doorway.

Xavier gently disengaged from the kiss and squeezed Lys's arms.

'Business calls,' he apologised ruefully.

Intoxicated by his kiss, Lys nodded. 'That's OK, I understand. I'll go to the café at the end and get a pizza, shall I?'

She returned and cut the pizza into slices and put them on the upturned box that served him as a table and sat on his bedroll, her back against the door, content to watch him at work.

Every so often, she strolled around

behind him to see what he had drawn, marvelling at his skill. She couldn't resist touching him as she stood by him. Just her fingertips on his shoulder seemed to draw electricity from his body to hers and she wondered if he felt it also.

Maybe he did. His eyes would momentarily leave the model and smile up at her. She couldn't help but notice the appreciative light in them and she longed for his sketching to be over so that they could spend some time alone together.

She knew she had to tell him about finding the necklace in her car. Whatever his reaction, she couldn't deceive him about it any longer.

When the moment came, after the last client had departed and he had tidied away his materials and tools, she wasn't sure how to begin.

'Shall we go to the restaurant for some supper?' Xavier suggested as he locked the door. 'I've done well today. If I had better clothes with me I would take you to the Hotel Paris.'

He drew her to him as he spoke, their foreheads pressed together. He gently kissed her lips.

Lys responded, but only half-heartedly, knowing she must delay no longer. 'I'm not hungry yet. Let's walk round the citadel for a while. I have something I must tell you.'

'Nothing is wrong, is it?' Xavier instantly asked, looking concerned. 'Your grandpère? He is all right?'

'What? Oh, yes, he's fine, though we have had some trouble I must tell you about later. No, this is something different, something between you and me.'

Xavier pulled her to him again as they approached the narrow metal footbridge that led over the narrow inlet to the inner harbour and across to the other side.

'If I didn't sense that your body is so in tune with mine, I would fear you were going to tell me that you no longer wanted to be my girl,' Xavier smiled, teasingly leaning down to nibble her ear as they strolled arm-in-arm across the bridge.

'Am I your girl?' Lys asked archly, revelling in the words.

Xavier's eyes gleamed darkly in the fading light. 'Of course!' he whispered into her ear. 'Didn't you know?'

Hmm! His *holiday* girl, nothing more! Still, wasn't that what they had agreed? She could hardly complain. She hadn't expected her emotions to become so deeply involved. But they had.

A wooden bench was positioned at the top of the path, strategically placed to overlook both the inner and outer harbours. Lys drew Xavier towards it and sat down.

Lys stared unseeingly over the harbour, wondering if her lack of trust of Xavier would bring an end to their friendship.

Xavier twisted sideways on the bench and gently touched her right cheek with the back of the fingers of his right hand. His other arm lay behind her shoulders and she could feel the warmth from it against her. As Xavier drew his fingers slowly down her cheek, Lys turned to face him and moved her lips against his fingers as she met his gaze.

'What is it?' he asked gently.

'I have your necklace,' she blurted out.

'Pardon?'

'Your necklace, you know, the diamond one.'

Xavier stared uncomprehendingly at her. He shook his head. 'I haven't got a diamond necklace.'

Lys returned his stare. 'Well, no, you haven't. I've got it. It was in my car, under the seat. I found it the other day when I cleaned my car. It's what the thugs were after.'

His face still looked blank and Lys added, 'It's like a collar. An intricate design with loops linking together and dangling down.'

'Where exactly did you find it?'

Xavier asked, a frown creasing his forehead.

He didn't look quite so blank about it now and Lys felt that he knew something about what she was describing.

'It was under the front passenger seat. I only found it when I decided to clean my car, and only you had been in besides myself.' She spread her hands helplessly. 'It can't have come there by any other means, unless someone deliberately hid it there — and that doesn't seem very likely. Even if it's a fake, it's still worth a lot of money — far too much to leave lying around.'

'Have you got it with you?'

'No. Like I said, it's too valuable to leave lying around.'

'Where is it, then?'

For some reason, Lys didn't want to give too much away, not yet. Xavier was acting a little strange, cautious, with unaccustomed hesitancy.

'I have it safe,' she temporised.

'And you aren't going to tell me where?'

It was a question — yet he spoke it more like a statement of fact.

Lys smiled to soften her words. 'Not unless you can tell me how it got into my car, and why you haven't wondered where it is.' She paused, then added, 'It could be what those men were after, except, if you didn't know you had it, why did they?'

Xavier looked thoughtful. 'Have you told anyone about it? The police, for example?'

Lys shook her head. 'Not yet. I thought I would try to find out who had left it there. After all, what could the police do about it? It hasn't been reported as stolen, and, if it were, it might be thought I'd stolen it.'

'How do you know it hasn't been reported as stolen?'

Lys shrugged. 'I sent a drawing of it to a friend who knows about such things. He told me.'

'And what did he tell you?'

Lys wasn't sure how much she should say. She was becoming more and more certain that Xavier knew something about it, and he wasn't letting on what. How much should she trust him?

'He said it looks like the Monsigny Collar, a priceless item a few centuries old. It could be a fake, though. I can't tell.'

She saw Xavier's face tighten. A tiny muscle twitched high on his cheekbone but he strove to keep in control of his features.

'If it is what your friend says,' he began carefully, 'it could be dangerous for you to keep it. If those men who attacked me believed that I had it in my possession and now know I don't, they might have been watching to see who I know here, and may suspect that I've given it to you.'

Lys nodded numbly. 'I know. That's why I wanted to know if you knew anything about it. However, since you don't, I think I had better hand it over to the police.'

Xavier's hand shot out to cover hers. 'Don't do that just yet. I . . .' He hesitated, then continued slowly, 'I do know something about it. I haven't stolen it,' he added quickly, 'but I have an idea how it might have got into my bag.'

He lapsed into silence for a few moments, obviously thinking about it. Lys wished he would take her into his full confidence but he didn't seem ready for that. Didn't he trust her? Did their friendship have much going for it if neither trusted the other?

Xavier squeezed her hand. 'You say it's somewhere safe?'

'Yes.'

He looked straight into her eyes. 'Do you trust me enough to show it to me?'

She returned his look. 'Do you trust me enough to tell me what you know?'

He smiled. 'Touché!'

He smiled again and considered for a moment. 'I can tell you that it belongs to . . . a relative of mine . . . and he feared it was about to be stolen. He asked me to take care of it but I refused. I knew I was coming here and didn't want the complication of such responsibility. It seems as though he must have put it into my bag whilst I was out of the room, and it tumbled out when I leaped into your car. I had been rummaging in the top for my water-proofs. I must have left the fastener undone.'

'It seems a bit careless of both of you, considering its value. Is it real?'

Xavier nodded. 'I . . . believe so.'

Lys's mind went into hyperactive mode. She had handled a priceless fortune! It was hidden in Grandpère's cottage. She was glad she had hidden it well.

Her thoughts must have been written on her face. Xavier gently took hold of her chin and turned her fully to face him again. She could read his concern for her in his expression.

'I really think it would be for the best if you were to give it back into my keeping. I don't want you involved in this.'

Did she trust him? Believe him? She thought so.

She nodded. 'All right, but what will you do with it?'

'I think I will have to go back h . . . to the mainland for a day or two, to sort it out.'

'How will you travel? You won't hitchhike with a fortune like that in your pocket, will you?'

'No.'

He looked at her carefully. 'Would you give me a lift to La Rochelle airport tomorrow? I'll make a call and reserve a seat, and, when I come back, I will tell you all about it, at least, as much as I can.'

So, there was still more? She thought as much! However, she felt she could go along with it so far. She was sure he wasn't a thief.

They returned to where Lys's car was parked. Xavier disappeared into the restaurant to make his phone call and came out bearing a box of chips and a variety of goujons of fish.

'Paul gave me these,' he grinned. 'Five more minutes won't make much difference. I'll bring my best suit back with me and I'll take you to the Hotel Paris when I return. You deserve it.'

They were back on their familiar footing and shared the box of food companionably in the two front seats of the car. Xavier's left arm held Lys close and they kissed and laughed together.

When the box was empty, Xavier tossed it onto the back seat.

'That's that! Come! We must go now. I won't rest until I know you are safely out of all this.'

Just what *all of this was*, Lys couldn't imagine. She trusted he would tell her as much as he was able afterwards.

It was less than twenty minutes later that they drew up on the rough land at the side of the windmill. Lys was alarmed to notice that the door of Grandpère's cottage was open. That shouldn't be.

She leapt out of her car without even switching off the engine and rushed inside the cottage. Although it was dark inside, there was enough light from the moon for her to see that the place had been turned upside down. The contents of the drawers and cupboards had been tipped out onto the floor; the coal bucket was upturned and empty, as was the vegetable rack, the flour bin, the tea and coffee caddies and the sugar pot.

In the same instant she thought of her grandfather. Had they harmed him? With his name of her lips she hurried forward, hardly aware of the sticky crunching under her feet as she sped across the room.

She could make out that Grandpère's bedroom was in similar chaos to the kitchen, but of Grandpère himself, there was no sign.

'Grandpère! Where are you?'

She felt her way forward, stepping carefully over the strewn bedclothes and emptied drawers, frantically feeling everything with her hands. He wasn't there.

Where was he? Was he lying injured somewhere? Or had they kidnapped him? Did they mean to hold him to ransom in return for the necklace?

Time seemed to stand still. Lys felt her chest tightening and thought she was going to faint.

She realised that Xavier was standing behind her and she turned to him, instinctively burying her face into him.

'He isn't here!' she muffled against his chest. Her body was shaking uncontrollably. She was aware of his arms strongly about her, holding her, comforting her.

Suddenly her body froze.

This had happened not twenty minutes after she had told Xavier that she had hidden the diamond necklace in the cottage. He had gone into the restaurant to phone his seat reservation on a flight from La Rochelle. Had he also phoned his conspirators to let them know where the necklace was hidden?

She stepped backwards, her hands pushing Xavier's chest, forcing him away from her, her lips almost soundlessly forming the word, 'No!'

'What is it?'

Xavier tried to pull her back to him but she resisted his efforts, straining her body away from him.

'What have you done?' she cried, horrified at her thoughts. 'He's not well! They'll kill him!'

She felt hysteria surging through her. She couldn't bear it if Grandpère had been hurt because of her misplaced trust in Xavier's innocence. She shouldn't have told him!

Xavier gripped her arms firmly just above her elbows and shook her slightly in his efforts to calm her.

'Lys! Listen to me! I had nothing to do with this! Nothing! Do you hear?'

Their eyes were getting used to the dark and Lys faced him, trying to focus on his face but it seemed to swim in and out of focus. She pushed his arm away and tried to go past him back into the kitchen.

He let her go and followed her, swinging her round to face him once more.

'Lys! Calm down. Let's look outside for him. He can't be far away!'

'They've taken him hostage! They'll bargain with us — Grandpère for the necklace! His heart won't stand it. We'll have to give them the necklace.'

'Stop and think, Lys! Where did you hide the necklace? Have they got it?'

'What? No, they can't have.' She looked around desperately trying to clear her mind. 'I don't know. I can't see it! They mustn't have, they wouldn't have taken Grandpère, would they?'

'Where did you put it?'

The simple question cleared her head and she stared at Xavier. She wanted to trust him, but how could she? He was the only other one who knew it was here.

Xavier took a step backwards. He held up the palms of his hands towards her.

'OK, Lys. It's OK! I understand. Look, I've got to go. I think I know who might have done this. I'll call the police and send them along. I'll be back tomorrow, or the day after. Trust me! I, I love you!'

He gripped her arms again and quickly kissed her lips, which were parted in shock. His words reverberated round her head. He loved her.

'Where . . . ?'

But he was gone.

10

'Lysette! Lysette! Are you there?' It was Madame Giraud's voice pulling Lys back to her senses. She stared at the older woman, who was now framed in the doorway. Her mind still felt too shocked to reply sensibly but she made an effort.

'Madame Giraud! Thank goodness!' She gestured with her outstretched arms. 'We've been burgled! Grandpère has gone!'

'He's with me, Lys. He's back in my cottage. It was a nasty shock for him but he had the sense to come straight back to me. Don't worry! He's all right! Really!'

She was smaller than Lys but, right then, she was a tower of strength. Her rounded body was a comforting cushion and Lys burst into tears with the relief of knowing Grandpère was all right.

'Come on, back with me,' Madame Giraud urged. 'Etienne is concerned about you and won't relax until he sees you. I've called the police. They will be here soon and will come to my cottage to find us.'

As Lys stumbled along at Madame Giraud's side, the older woman kept up a stream of chatter, no doubt to give Lys time to recover from the shock.

'They must have had the effrontery to do it in broad daylight, or near enough! I don't know what the world is coming to, I don't!'

'But, I don't understand,' Lys finally managed to falter. 'In daylight?'

She hadn't told Xavier about the necklace until dusk had fallen. He couldn't have phoned anyone. She had misjudged him entirely.

'What time did it happen? Do you know?'

'We don't know exactly. It was already done when Etienne returned home after supper. It was a bit late for him, after nine o'clock. He walked straight into it. Luckily for him, they had already gone. Or it might have been far worse.

Etienne looked shaken but his voice was steady and he rose to hug Lys as she entered the room.

'You mark by words, it's that Leon Boudot, getting back at us!' he predicted after Lys had sat down beside him on the two-seater sofa. 'I bet he's had a right old rollicking off his boss. Wouldn't be surprised to hear he's lost his job. Serve him right, too.'

'Leon Boudot?' Lys echoed. 'What has he . . . ? Oh, I see what you mean.'

That business had long gone from her brain. She pondered on it for a moment but shook her head.

'I don't think so, Grandpère. He wouldn't dare. He'd be more subtle than that.'

Her mind was busy filtering through the other alternative. Although Xavier hadn't had time to tell anyone about the necklace being there, he might have been right about the men who attacked

165

him having been keeping watch. Which meant he was involved in some way. Was his story true about a relative asking him to look after the necklace?

It seemed a bit far-fetched. Robert had said it belonged to the Monsigny family. Was Xavier a long-distant cousin or something? He could be, she mused. He'd said his name was Piquet. If she'd had cousins on her mother's side of the family, they wouldn't be called Dupont.

So what was she to tell the police when they came?

In the end, she didn't mention any of their theories, because that was all they were, theories. The police took some flash photographs, said that as nothing had been damaged or stolen it must have been an opportunist attempt to find something of value, and warned them to be careful and not go out leaving the door open.

Lys hadn't had the opportunity to check if the diamond necklace was still there, but when she did so, it was. She smiled grimly. And there it would stay until she had a believable account of its history.

They were tired. Madame Giraud pointed out that Etienne had suffered enough shock for one day and insisted that he stayed with her in her second bedroom. The bed was already made up she said, adding, 'And you, too, Lysette. You can't go back into all that mess tonight. We can make up a bed on the sofa, I'm sure.'

Lys shook her head. 'Thank you, madame, but I would rather sleep at home. I would only lie here worrying in case they came back. Don't worry. I won't try to tidy it up tonight, and I'll make myself very secure.'

Which she did, by pulling the kitchen table across the barred door. Then she quickly re-made her bed and was soon snuggled down in it. She lay awake for a while, wondering if Xavier would return as he had promised. Would he only return when he knew for sure that the thieves hadn't got the necklace? The thought of his possible complicity depressed her greatly.

She awakened just after nine o'clock and spent the next hour tidying up the kitchen and throwing out the ruined flour, sugar and other commodities. She salvaged some fruit for her breakfast and tried her uttermost to be cheerful as she worked, although, inside, she felt low in spirit. She knew it was a reaction to the previous evening's events and the uncertainties of the future of her friendship with Xavier.

She sighed deeply. She had misjudged him over the imagined phone call. She hoped she were still misjudging him. Would he forgive her, or was it over between them?

And what was truth about it all? Xavier himself hadn't been all that open with her. What was his connection with the attempted theft?

Lys spent all of Sunday and Monday tidying up the mess in the cottage, thankful that her grandfather was content to remain at Madame Giraud's cottage until their home was habitable once more. She took the opportunity to give the cottage a thorough cleaning.

On Tuesday morning she replenished the spoiled groceries and felt reasonably content that the cottage was fit for her grandfather to return home to before he got too used to the comforts of Madame Giraud's home.

A surprise visit from the municipal clerk brought the exciting news that their application for a grant had been presented to a council meeting the previous evening and, in consideration of the irregularities that had occurred, the decision had been rushed through, and the award granted. There was nothing to stop them proceeding with their plans.

Lys rushed round to the patisserie to share the news. Everything was beginning to go so well, everything except her relationship with Xavier.

After lunch, Lys left Etienne having an afternoon snooze in Madame Giraud's armchair. In mid-afternoon, the sound of the heavy pounding of rotor blades beating the air drew her to the cottage doorway. She gasped in amazement. A helicopter was hovering just overhead and it was going to land by the windmill.

She shaded her eyes with her hand and gazed up at the cockpit. The pilot was wearing a flying helmet with earphones but there was something familiar about him. He raised a hand in salute. It couldn't be! Xavier had returned.

The helicopter landed smoothly in the space that was destined to be their car park and the engine was cut. Lys stared as Xavier jumped to the ground, bending low under the still-revolving blades. She wanted to run to him, but her feet seemed rooted to the ground. She watched as he turned to give a helping hand to an older man. Not that he needed it. The man jumped down and straightened his suit.

He seemed to be aged between forty and fifty, Lys guessed. His hair was beginning to grey but that only added to his air of sophisticated charm. Lys had no doubts but that he was Xavier's father, and here she was in her old jeans and T-shirt with a sweeping brush in her hand.

Xavier turned to face her. He seemed different. Of course. He was dressed in a casual suit, though, as he removed his flying helmet, his familiar dreadlocks tumbled into view. Was the suit a sign that he wasn't staying? It seemed like an unspoken message that he didn't belong here any more.

The two men walked towards her. Xavier was speaking to his father. His arm indicated the windmill and then the cottage and Lys presumed he was saying something of what she and her grandfather were hoping to achieve.

And then, he was just a couple of metres away.

Lys's heart was pounding. It all seemed too formal, and out of her league. Xavier had flown the helicopter. His father oozed wealth. Even Xavier looked like a city-dweller. Where were his fraying cut-off jeans and scruffy T-shirt?

Xavier halted and smiled a little uncertainly. 'I came back, as I promised,' he said softly.

'Yes,' Lys acknowledged noncommittally. Unsure of what this flamboyant arrival meant, she didn't know what else to say.

Xavier, too, seemed more constrained than usual. 'I've brought someone to meet you,' he said. 'May I present my father, Comte de Monsigny. Papa, I present Mademoiselle Lys Dupont.'

Lys swallowed. Comte de Monsigny! Xavier's father?

Bewildered, she held out her hand.

The Comte took hold of it and bowed formally. 'Enchanté, mademoiselle!'

His grey eyes twinkled at her, surprising her with their warmth. 'I believe my son has a lot of explaining to do. I have come to vouch for him and, more seriously, to apologise for the activities of my elder son, Henri.'

'Monsieur?'

Was that how one addressed a Comte? She didn't know! She looked from father to son, her emotions still in turmoil. She might have misjudged him, but he had allowed her to think he was a penniless artist, working for a meagre living. Not the son of a count. Why had he deceived her?

She squirmed with embarrassment as she thought of the times she had offered to buy him food. Why had he pretended to be poor? She felt belittled, ridiculed. Had he been laughing at her efforts?

The Comte's reference to his elder son sank into her mind and she immediately pulled her attention back to him. The Comte implied that his other son was implicated in the burglary. He, also, would be torn between emotions, she surmised, with shame for his elder son's behaviour being uppermost at present.

Remembering the niceties of life, she

invited the two men into the cottage, glad that it was presentable once more.

Xavier and his father stood behind the two chairs that Lys indicated, waiting until she had seated herself in a third.

Xavier reached out towards Lys's hands, which she had clasped in front of her, resting on the table. Fearful of the ready response she might make, she swiftly withdrew them, wishing she didn't have the overpowering urge to be gathered in his arms.

He grinned sheepishly. 'I've, er, been less than honest with you, Lys. I'm sorry. It wasn't deliberate deception. I really am an artist and I came here to spend the summer sketching and painting on the island. I enjoy the simple rustic style of life, I like to live side by side with other artists. There are fewer complications, usually.'

'You said your name was Piquet. That was deliberate deception,' Lys said coldly.

'It is my mother's family name. We often use it.'

'You must have had fun listening to me gabbling on about what you could or couldn't afford. I thought you were poor, eking out a living sketching people's portraits. Why didn't you say you are the son of a Count and could probably afford to buy the whole island?'

Xavier laughed. 'Hardly!'

He cast an amused glance at his father, and then back to Lys. 'Sure, I had a privileged upbringing, but I now support myself. I am the younger son,' he hastened to add. 'I had to learn to make my own way in life. My brother inherits the title and all that goes with it, if there's anything left by then.'

'What do you mean?' Lys was intrigued, in spite of her pique.

Xavier's father leaned forward. He smiled wryly. 'Maybe, if I take over here, mademoiselle. You see my elder son, Henri, has no intention of soiling his hands in any form of honest endeavour. He knows that, at some point of his life, maybe he hopes sooner rather than later, he will inherit our family fortune, a fortune I have sustained by running a successful stable and stud farm. Unfortunately, Henri has already started to spend it, in disastrously large amounts. Even more unfortunate . . . '

He paused and seemed to find the words hard to say. His face looked bleak and Lys felt sorry for him.

He sighed. 'Henri has been selling family treasures that are irreplaceable. He visits my home and suddenly something else has gone!'

Lys was shocked.

The Comte waved his hand in a resigned gesture.

'Take no heed, mademoiselle. It has become a way of life. Henri has gone through it all. Drugs, alcohol abuse, gambling, illegal syndicates, who knows what else?'

'And he had his eye on the diamond collar?'

'Yes. Foolishly, or should I say, fortunately, he wasn't content with the underworld price he had been offered and he contacted a well-known jeweller who happens to be a particular friend of mine. Jacques phoned to query his statement that I was the true vendor and that he was simply my agent.'

'Why didn't you just leave it in your bank or in a hidden safe, somewhere where he couldn't find it?'

'He would lie, forge my signature, anything to get what he wants. He knows I won't shame our name by disclosing his thefts, though, this time, he has gone too far. Besides, he knew the necklace was at home.

'When Xavier called on his way here, I was desperate to keep it out of Henri's hands. What I didn't know was that Xavier was also calling to see Henri. During their conversation, he mentioned he had taken his leave of me earlier that day, and when Henri later realised that I no longer had the collar he put two and two together, and sent his henchmen to take it by force.'

'Except I had carelessly lost it,' Xavier put in ruefully. 'And didn't even know it.'

'And I couldn't think of any good reason why you should have such an expensive piece of jewellery in your possession,' Lys admitted, relaxing her guard with him for the first time since his return. 'I wondered if it might have belonged to Jocelyn, but even that didn't make real sense.'

'How has Jocelyn been involved?' the Count asked.

'Lys and her grandfather needed an urgent independent survey made on their windmill, so I asked Jocelyn to break into her holiday, which she did. Hasn't she mentioned it?'

'Maybe to your mother but not to me. I hope you didn't take advantage of your sister's position, Xavier.'

'Sister?' Lys echoed, visibly bristling. How much more deceit had he employed against her?

Xavier grinned at her. 'Didn't I say?'

178

'No, you did not!'

The Comte coughed discreetly, drawing their attention away from each other. 'Perhaps if Mademoiselle Dupont would tell us where she put the diamond collar for safe-keeping?' he suggested mildly. He reached into the inside pocket of his jacket and drew out his passport.

'This is proof of my identity, mademoiselle.' He smiled. 'I would not want you to hand over our family heirloom to anyone, not even myself, without checking that I am who I say I am.'

Lys glanced at it, though she knew she had no need. His sincerity was evident.

'That's fine. I believe you.'

Her eyes narrowed slightly as she glanced sideways at his son, still smarting at his deception.

'The necklace is here, monsieur. It is safe.'

'Here? Henri's men missed it?'

Lys nodded. 'I knew I couldn't just

leave something so valuable lying around. I suppose I knew there was a possibility of them coming here.'

She grinned mischievously. 'If I gave you a whole day in here, I don't think you would find it.'

Xavier looked around at the simple interior of the cottage, shaking his head as he remembered the chaos the burglars left behind.

'Did you bury it outside?'

Lys laughed outright, her annoyance temporarily forgotten. 'No! It's in here!'

She directed her glance to the bare stone wall above the door lintel.

Xavier and his father followed her glance. They could see nothing, only the stonework. Xavier rose from his seat and stood under the lintel. He reached up and touched the wood, but it seemed solid.

Lys handed him a heavy kitchen knife. 'Prise that stone from the wall!'

With a puzzled look, Xavier jabbed in the point of the knife where Lys pointed and twisted it, loosening a layer of stone. As he pulled it completely away and turned it in his hands, a look of understanding came into his eyes. It was too light in weight. It wasn't stone.

'I remembered how you prepared your canvasses and how hard they became,' Lys explained. 'So, I wrapped the necklace in layers of tin-foil, then covered it in pottery clay. When it had hardened, I covered it with layers of duck and painted on layers of gesso to harden it, so that it looked like a piece of stone. Then, I rolled it in the dust and stuck it on the wall, on view to all — seen but unseen.'

Xavier and his father looked at her in admiration. 'It couldn't have been in better hands!' The Comte smiled.

Having decided not to risk damaging the precious collar by hacking its protective covering apart without due care, it lay on the table in front of them whilst the Comte asked interested questions about the windmill museum project but, eventually, he stood to take his leave.

'My grateful thanks once again, Mademoiselle Dupont,' the Comte smiled, bowing over Lys's hand once more, 'but I must take my leave of you. We have guests at home and I must return to them.'

Lys's heart felt bleak. So this was it, then. Xavier would leave with his father. He already looked the part of a city dweller. Maybe he would stay there to support his father in his dealings with the elder brother?

Xavier held open the cottage door and then followed them out into the sunshine. Silently, they headed over towards the parked helicopter. At about twenty metres away, Xavier touched her arm.

'This is near enough,' he warned. 'Stay here.'

As he moved forward, Lys felt as though her heart was breaking. He wasn't even going to say good-bye! Just a curt, 'Stay here!' She felt a lump in her throat and only her pride stopped her from turning away and running back to the protective dim interior of the cottage.

She saw the two men shake hands and briefly embrace, but it was only when the Comte climbed into the pilot's seat and Xavier raised his hand in salute and then walked back towards her that she realised with a stab of joy that Xavier wasn't accompanying him.

'You're not going?'

Xavier took hold of her hands. 'Of course not! We have a bit of celebrating to do. Why do you think I wore my suit? Didn't I say I would take you to the Hotel Paris when I returned?'

He looked at her tenderly, amazed at the effect she had on him. No strings, he'd said, but now, when he thought of what might have happened to her had she been in the cottage when Henri's men arrived, he wanted to bind her to him for life.

He took hold of her hands. Regardless of his father's presence, he drew her hands to his lips and kissed her fingertips.

'Forgive me?' he asked softly. 'I simply meant to have an uncomplicated summer amongst other artists, I didn't know I was going to meet someone who would rock the foundations of my life.'

Lys looked at him with surprise. 'Did I?'

He smiled tenderly. 'Like a storm!'

Her parted lips seemed like an invitation to kiss them and Xavier softly covered them with his own, savouring her sweetness for an inestimable time. Neither was aware of the sound of the helicopter's engine bursting into life, nor its departure. When eventually their lips eased apart, they lingered forehead-to-forehead, reluctant to lose contact with each other.

'So, is it a date?'

'You'll spoil your image if any of your artistic friends see you.'

'I'll risk it! Tonight we'll dine like royalty, and tomorrow I'll resume my rustic image. We both have a busy summer ahead of us. You with your windmill, and I with my painting.'

She could already feel the windmill's sails turning in the wind, and she sensed her future with Xavier would be more than a dream. Still, she didn't have to make it too easy for him, did she? After all, he had deceived her a little!

'I'll think about it,' she breathed softly, raising her lips once more to his, and, to make sure his lips lingered longer than previously, she twined her fingers into his hair and held him close, and all rational thoughts sailed away.

THE END

We do hope that you have enjoyed reading this large print book.

Did you know that all of our titles are available for purchase?

We publish a wide range of high quality large print books including:
Romances, Mysteries, Classics
General Fiction
Non Fiction and Westerns

Special interest titles available in large print are:
The Little Oxford Dictionary
Music Book, Song Book
Hymn Book, Service Book

Also available from us courtesy of Oxford University Press:
Young Readers' Dictionary
(large print edition)
Young Readers' Thesaurus
(large print edition)

For further information or a free brochure, please contact us at:
Ulverscroft Large Print Books Ltd.,
The Green, Bradgate Road, Anstey,
Leicester, LE7 7FU, England.
Tel: (00 44) **0116 236 4325**
Fax: (00 44) **0116 234 0205**